Zephaniah Moore Humphrey, Henry Neill

Memorial Sketches - Heman Humphrey - Sophia Porter Humphrey

Zephaniah Moore Humphrey, Henry Neill

Memorial Sketches - Heman Humphrey - Sophia Porter Humphrey

ISBN/EAN: 9783337013820

Printed in Europe, USA, Canada, Australia, Japan

Cover: Foto ©Raphael Reischuk / pixelio.de

More available books at **www.hansebooks.com**

MEMORIAL SKETCHES.

HEMAN HUMPHREY.

SOPHIA PORTER HUMPHREY.

PHILADELPHIA:
J. B. LIPPINCOTT & CO.
1869.

LIPPINCOTT'S PRESS, PHILADELPHIA.

HEMAN HUMPHREY.

TO THE GRANDCHILDREN OF HEMAN AND
SOPHIA PORTER HUMPHREY.

———————

WHEN, in 1861, your grandfather died, his
sons projected an extended Memoir of his
life and times. The execution of the project was
delayed by the ill-health of two of those by whom
the work was assumed. Then came the civil war,
which so completely absorbed the public attention
that we felt constrained to wait until a more tranquil
period for a hearing : our story was too quiet for
stormy times. Then death deprived us of the most
graceful pen upon which we had relied. Then the
whole work was committed to the son-in-law whose
initials are here appended. He had scarcely gathered his materials when the grandmother followed
her husband into the other world. Then the Me-

1 *

moir was laid aside for the present Memorial, which, though it be but an imperfect outline of two precious lives, is, at least, better than a mere monumental inscription. Its familiar cast will, we hope, make it more acceptable to you than any statelier delineation could be. Should no elaborate memoir of either grandparent ever be printed, this will remind you of ancestral virtues, and teach you of that which makes one's life a priceless legacy.

Z. M. H.

H. N.

Heman Humphrey.

I.

A PERFECT biography can never be written: an outline of a human life can be drawn, but it will be scarcely better than one of the first rude sketches of a master in art—distinct, but wanting in that detail which is essential to the finished picture. A perfect portrait, indeed, is impossible, though the artist should exhaust the resources of form and color. The painter works to an ideal; and when he has succeeded in the expression of that ideal, he has left unexpressed very much which characterizes his subject. The biographer has this advantage: that he may present a series of sketches, a gallery of portraits, representing his subject in varying moods and under varying conditions; but he can never reproduce the innumerable touches of detail which are essential to the perfection of each of his sketches.

The Memorial herein presented, does not profess

to be even a biography. It is roughly and imperfectly drawn, rather as a suggestion than as a completed work. It is a memorial to those for whom it is prepared, because reminding them of a life with which they were familiar. They will readily supply, from their own memories, many of the details which are omitted. Thus the life may stand out to them in much of its rounded beauty, however imperfect may be the memorial in itself considered.

We are fortunate in having the materials of our present work abundantly provided in posthumous papers, among the most important of which are somewhat voluminous autobiographical sketches, whose fresh tints will be continually employed. These sketches were written by their author in leisure hours, near the close of his life, at the request of his children. They were composed in no ambitious mood, but in that of a man sitting down in the evening of his days to talk with his family of the incidents of his career. This will appear in the style which clothes the quotations we shall make from them. They are to us the more charming on account of their homely simplicity. Indeed, we would be glad to retain the familiar quality of the fireside talk in all these pages, for they are intended only for partial eyes. Should they be read by any to whom their subject was unknown, this intention will not be forgotten. Read in the spirit in which it was prepared, this memorial may perhaps give any one some vivid impressions of a life whose perfect record is in heaven only; the whole of whose earthly influences can no more be traced by us, than can those of a stream, which runs into the countless leaves and fruits it nourishes along its course, as well as into the broad sea in which it loses itself at last.

II.

THE life of HEMAN HUMPHREY may be considered as a representative life. It covered a period of transition. It began when society in New England bore the type of Puritan culture. It ended when that type had almost disappeared in the American culture of to-day. It began when a clergyman's parish was a township—when, in many villages, all were taxed for the support of the Gospel, irrespective of creed. The "meeting-house" of the day was a central rallying-spot and the focus of influence. The "minister" had all interests—religious, social, educational, and even political—very much under his control. He was regarded by all with a respect and reverence at present rarely accorded to his successors. In that day the "tithing-man" was an important functionary in the house of God. With a long staff in hand, he busied himself during the hours of worship in controlling the too-wakeful children in the gallery, and in arousing the too-drowsy adults in the pews "below." An hour-glass often stood upon the pulpit, and was solemnly turned by the preacher as he began his sermon. It was frequently turned again before he had ended. The square pews of the "meeting-house" were uncarpeted and uncushioned. The seats were hinged, so that when the audience rose for prayer, the wooden leaves could be raised and thrown back against the high parapets of the pews. No heating apparatus except the "foot-stove" was allowed in the sanctuary. A modern furnace would then have been considered no less a heresy than an organ in the place of public worship. A shelter from wind and storm, was luxury enough for those whose ancestors first offered their public devotions under the pine trees of Plymouth in the winter season.

The dwellings of those days were generally plain, if not absolutely rude. The more substantial farmhouses were framed with solid timbers. An idea of the prevailing style of domestic architecture may still be gained by the traveler in New England, from some weatherbeaten structure, covered by a "gambrel" roof, sloping backward at the rear almost to the ground. The sides, as well as the roofs of these old houses, were often protected by shingles, thus reminding one of Norman soldiers encased in scale-plated armor. The kitchen, with its wide fireplace, was the favorite resort of the family. The "keeping-room" was used in the later hours of the day. The parlor was opened only upon "state occasions." The loom occupied some convenient corner, and the spinning-wheel was always ready to be set in the firelight of winter, or in the shades of summer. Many glimpses of prevailing habits and ideas will be gained by those who glance through the following pages. So also, the gradual change which those habits and ideas underwent in the progress of a long life, will be observed.

III.

HEMAN HUMPHREY was born in West Simsbury, now Canton, Hartford county, Connecticut, March 26, 1779. His father's name was SOLOMON HUMPHREY, descended in direct line from MICHAEL HUMPHREY, who came to this country from England some time previous to 1643, and among whose numerous relatives and descendants are found many of distinguished name; such as

Thomas Dudley, Governor of the Massachusetts Colony for seventeen years, and William Leete, Governor and Deputy Governor for many years of the New Haven Colony. " Piety and integrity are general characteristics of those in this line of descent, whose names have never become famous." In 1647, Michael Humphrey, having then become a resident of Windsor, Connecticut, married PRISCILLA GRANT, daughter of a merchant of Windsor. Of seven children, born of this marriage, SAMUEL was the third: born, 1656. He married Mary, daughter of Samuel Mills, and died in 1736, aged eighty years. His third son, JONATHAN, married MARY, daughter of Rev. Benjamin Ruggles, of Suffield. From this marriage descended SOLOMON, third son, who settled in West Simsbury, and there married NAOMI, daughter of Brewster Higley. The third son of Solomon Humphrey bore his own name. He was born in 1747, and married a second wife, HANNAH, daughter of Capt. John Brown, of West Simsbury. The first issue of this marriage was HEMAN, the subject of this memorial.

When the historic Mayflower cast anchor in Plymouth harbor, December, 1620, on the list of her passengers stood the name of PETER BROWN. To this member of that famous band of emigrants was born a son, to whom he gave his own name.

This son is believed to have left Plymouth with a colony of settlers who removed to what became the Windsor alluded to above. A tombstone still standing in the town of Old Windsor bears the name of Peter Brown, and a date (1692) which corresponds with our theory. A tradition cherished in the family lends corroborative evidence. From the last-named PETER BROWN, was descended the mother of Heman Humphrey.

Her father, Capt. John Brown, died in the service of his country during the war of the Revolution, having hastened with his company of volunteers to the defence of New York. He expired in camp on Haarlem Heights, June, 1776, aged forty-eight years.

Hannah was the eldest of his children, and at his death was eighteen years of age. The widow was left in stinted circumstances, on a rough farm, with eleven children. She was, however, a woman of remarkable strength of character, and exhibited an uncommon degree of energy, fortitude and discretion in conducting her farm and in rearing her children during the trying period of the war.

Solomon Humphrey, the husband of Hannah, is described as a man of " good common-school education ; of a more than ordinary taste for reading ; of good sense and unblemished moral character,

2

temperate, industrious and frugal." He resided in
West Simsbury until 1755, at which time he removed to Bristol; thence in 1813 to Barkhamstead,
where he died in 1834. His occupation was that
of a farmer. He had a numerous family of children—fourteen in all. Three of them died in early
childhood. Eleven of them lived to adult age,
several still surviving. Their names are HORACE
and SOLOMON, born of his first wife; HEMAN,
LUCY, LUTHER, CLARINDA, CANDACE, NAOMI,
HANNAH, ELECTA and HARRIET.

The mother of this large family was a woman
of uncommon mental capacity, and eagerly read
such books as could be obtained. The number of
these, however, was very small. "For years we
had not half a dozen on the shelf, except the Bible,
the Assembly's Catechism and the spelling-book."
She did what she could for the education of her
children, and did not fail to instruct them in that
standard compend of doctrine—the Catechism—each
Sunday, "after meeting."

IV.

THE first seminary into which Heman was introduced was a *barn*. It was, however, in summer days. The flail stood in the corner, and the

swallows made nests for themselves among the rafters. The little scholar was perched upon a high bench, and learned the alphabet and some of Dr. Watts' Hymns for Infant Minds. " I have a dim recollection of acting in an infant dialogue prepared for the entertainment of visitors."

He was about six years of age when his father removed to Bristol. There the opportunities afforded for instruction were slender. For three years the mother taught the little ones as she had time, her manuals being Dilworth's Spelling-Book and the Bible. The story of David and Goliath was one of the first of her Scripture lessons. Then followed the twelfth chapter of Ecclesiastes, which young Heman committed to memory.

" When I was nine or ten years old, we had a winter school (as it was called), kept by a neighbor, for a few weeks, in his own house. He was a small farmer, of no education, and of the very flattest Yankee pronunciation. His shaggy eyebrows, his frown, his heavy stamp, which made the rickety floor tremble, and his rude ' ferule,' are about the only things of his administration which I remember. The next winter, another neighbor, more skilled in catching trout than in teaching, took the pedagogical chair. He had a little smattering of common-school learning ; but was, if possible, a still flatter Yankee than his predecessor. Of thin visage, sharp voice, and with long birch whip and heavy ferule, he tried to keep us in order, to lead us along in ' Dilworth,' and to teach some of the older boys the art of writing. To do him justice, he was a very good penman for those times. As paper was scarce and dear, he used white birch-bark for his ' copies.' "

A better teacher was Mr. Simeon Hart, to whom Heman was sent in his thirteenth year. In Mr. Hart's school he passed four successive winters, when he supposed he had *finished* his education. How complete that education was, we may understand when we hear him say, " I knew almost nothing of geography as taught by globe and map, was but indifferently versed in the higher rules of arithmetic, and knew nothing of English grammar, except a little found in one of the earlier editions of Webster's Spelling-Book. I had never parsed a sentence. Thus scantily furnished, I expected to go forth and make my way in some humble employment.

" I was from childhood fond of reading ; but my difficulty was to find anything to read, except the New England Primer, Robinson Crusoe and The Pilgrim's Progress. We took no newspaper. Indeed, there was none to take, except the *Connecti-*

cut Courant, which was printed on a very small sheet, and which rarely found its way into our retired and humble parish."

Before long, however, a small library was collected under the auspices of the pastor of the parish. To this our " educated" boy had access, and soon read many of its volumes, chiefly histories, by the light of pine torches or of the kitchen fire.

V.

WHILE this educational process was going on in successive winters, the summers were occupied in manual labor upon his father's farm. When the education was " finished," he left home and placed himself in the employ of a neighbor. He was then seventeen years of age. It indicates his physical strength and skill that during this first summer as " hired man," he reaped and bound an acre of wheat in one day.

During the next summer he was employed at higher wages, by a Mr. Cowles, of Farmington; so also during the following summer. Here he learned much of the art of husbandry. His taste for reading was gratified by the *Connecticut Courant.* " I well remember how impatiently I used to wait for the post-rider to bring it, and how

eagerly I read it—advertisements and all." Here
also he learned his first lessons in temperance, dis-
covering that he could endure the heat and toil of
the harvest-field better without alcoholic drinks than
with them.

His fourth summer away from home was spent
with Governor Treadwell, of Farmington. "I can
never be sufficiently thankful for the kind Providence which gave me a home in his inestimable
family. I now see him as he rode up to my father's
door, on a fine horse, to engage me for the summer.
I need not say that he was a Puritan of the old
school, and in every way worthy to succeed Governor Trumbull in the highest office in the State.
He was not a man of quick parts and popular
address; but of a clear, logical, comprehensive
mind and solid judgment. He was a Christian, and
an exceedingly able theologian, as well as an able
judge and an incorruptible statesman. During the
summer I spent in his employ, he was one of the
principal writers in the *New York Theological
Magazine;* and some of his metaphysical articles
would have done no discredit to President Edwards
himself. He was very kind to me, and gave me
the free use of his library, which, though not very
large, helped me to the reading of many volumes.
As we went to our work early and returned early,

I had an hour before dark almost every day for reading. Occasionally I used to carry a book, or inkstand and sheet of paper into the field, and read or write a little, while the cattle were ' baiting' at the ' noon-spell;' sometimes using the cart for my shade, and the ' hind-board' for a desk."

The following summer was spent in Newington. The summer succeeding this, he expected to spend in the employ of Governor Treadwell; but being detained in his journey to Farmington by a freshet, he found, when he reached the house of Governor Treadwell, that he had already engaged all the help he desired. With inexpressible disappointment the young farmer returned to his father's home; being led by a way which he knew not.

VI.

THE intervals between these five summers of farm-life were spent in teaching school. "My first essay in this line was while in my seventeenth year. I taught three months at seven dollars per month, and ' boarded 'round.' My school was held in one of the front rooms of a one-story private house. The other front room and the kitchen were in the closest proximity, so that the pupils could hear all that was going on in the family." The three following winters were spent in teaching in three separate districts of Burlington.

Thrown upon his own resources by the failure of his engagement with Governor Treadwell, he was encouraged by his pastor, Rev. Jonathan Miller, to occupy the summer in study. He was then twenty years old. Mr. Miller volunteered to give him some instruction in the rudiments of Latin, suggesting the hope, which seemed almost as wild as a dream, that perhaps Mr. Humphrey might one day become a minister. A Latin grammar was procured. A little knowledge of English syntax was acquired, and the study of the Latin began. The health of the student soon suffered from the confinement of unremitted application. Two months were spent in the harvest-field. Then to study again. Then to teaching through the winter. Then once more to the Latin: Once again to the harvest-field. Once more to the school-house and to the books of study. And so the process went on until the spring of 1803, when Mr. Humphrey was advised by one of his clerical friends—in Harwinton, where his later labors as teacher were pursued—to make an effort to enter the Junior class of Yale College in the succeeding autumn.

Before following him to that institution, we must pause by the path we have been traversing to speak more at length of his experiences in the school-room and of his religious development.

VII.

THE low standard of common-school instruction in that day, in Connecticut, has already been spoken of. Strange as it may seem, one of the teacher's greatest difficulties arose from the magnitude of the Common-School Fund of the State. This Fund, the result of land sales on the "Western Reserve," Ohio, increased gradually to two millions of dollars. Taxes for the support of schools were made lighter and lighter, until the people, learning to depend upon the Fund, would not contribute even to make up its small deficiencies. They "began to calculate, in many places, for how many months the dividends would pay the teachers, at the lowest wages; and to content themselves with raising but little by tax, subscription, or any other means." Thus, what should have been only a help, was, through some not very obscure law of human nature, only a hindrance.

"Those who are now young can scarcely conceive the disadvantages under which we labored—teachers and scholars, both—a half century ago. Webster's Spelling-Book and 'Third Part,' The

Columbian Reader and Dwight's small Geography
were about all our class-books. Such a thing as a
blackboard, or apparatus of any kind, was never
thought of. And what shall I say of the school-
houses? So small and low, so miserably fitted up
and warmed were most of them, that it was a real
penance to be shut up in them six mortal hours
each day. There was not one comfortable seat for
the little sufferers, who were huddled together in the
smallest space, leaving scarcely room for the teacher's table to stand anywhere. Outside, there was
no wood-shed; not even a screen of boards." All
shade trees had been carefully taken from the vicinity. "It was not uncommon, when we came on the
appointed day to open our schools, to find everything in a ruinous condition—doors off the hinges;
glass out; benches broken; dirt accumulated every-
where; perhaps not a stick of wood for a fire. A
neighbor or two might be there with hammer and
saw, with putty and three-cornered pieces of tin,
taking out the windows, mending the doors, the long
writing-desks and the slab benches ; promising,
meanwhile, that some one should bring a load of
firewood before night. Many a time, through the
winter, some of us had to *dig out* our fuel—so
called—from beneath the snow-drifts, and to set the
boys to reducing it from ' sled length' to the proper

dimensions; that we might not freeze, if indeed the 'fuel' would burn when it was prepared. Sometimes our schools must be dismissed for a day or two, because we had no wood at all."

Having all these difficulties to contend with, Mr. Humphrey and some of his fellow-teachers in the vicinity, formed an association for mutual improvement. Few of them had any early advantages except of the slenderest kind. With one exception, none of them had ever enjoyed the instruction afforded by an academy, or by any of the higher schools of the day. As an association, they were accustomed to spend an evening together once in two or three weeks. Their object was to report successes, discuss difficulties, compare methods and consider new plans of effort. At these meetings they also introduced critical exercises in reading, both in prose and poetry; settling questions of accent or pronunciation by an appeal to the highest authority within their reach—Webster's Spelling-Book.

They also adopted the expedient of school visitation. The plan was, for each teacher to suspend the ordinary exercises of his school for half a day, occasionally, that, with his larger scholars, he might visit some neighboring school. The visit was made without previous notice; and was designed to give the pupils an idea of the relative excellences or defects of all the schools in the neighborhood.

"It is difficult for any one who has never witnessed it, to conceive the healthful emulation with which it inspired both teachers and pupils; how eagerly the visitor-boys watched every movement in the school; how they listened to every class in reading and spelling; and with what interest they talked about the visit for days and weeks afterward."

Great efforts were made, also, to induce parents and friends to visit the schools. "Sometimes, a little notice would bring in half the district of an afternoon. When the people grew remiss, we took care to remind them how much we relied upon the stimulus of their more frequent visits; and such appeals were generally successful. In this way we kept up an interest in our schools, which we could not have secured by any other method."

"Then again, at the close of the winter schools, we had what we called our 'quarter days,' when we brought half a dozen or more schools together in the meeting-house, for exercises in spelling, declamation and dialogue. These were great days with our scholars, and with their parents. The house was filled. Every one was there, and all came to be pleased and to see which school did the best. It required some time to prepare for these occasions; but no part of the term was spent to better advantage."

It seems to have been customary to close each of these exhibitions with a brief address by one of the teachers. We find among the papers of Mr. Humphrey two or three addresses prepared by himself for this purpose. From one of them we quote somewhat extensively, as therein a vivid idea is conveyed of the manner in which the more dramatic part of these entertainments was conducted. Some objection appears to have been made to this feature of the exhibitions, especially as they were given in the "meeting-house." This objection is briefly considered, and disposed of by the plea that all the dialogues had been carefully expurgated; and that wit and humor were used only for the purpose of exposing vice, and of elevating the moral standard of the community. "And now, in view of all this, and when it is considered that no other place will conveniently accommodate a large collection of people, can any one seriously object to such exhibitions in the meeting-house? Does it harm the building? All public business is done in this house, and against that no objection is made. Why then should it be thought so very criminal for schools to meet here once or twice in a year; and in a decent,

3

orderly manner give specimens of their learning and proof of their activity."

He then recapitulates the exercises of the evening.

" Several of the introductory pieces, which were very short, and spoken by our smallest scholars, were designed rather to amuse than to inform ; yet we conceive them not to be entirely destitute of moral instruction. The little orator, who assumes as much importance as if he were master of all the eloquence of Greece and Rome, does not stand alone. How often do we see persons giving themselves airs of superiority upon subjects of which they are as profoundly ignorant as is a boy of three feet high of the boldest flights of rhetoric !"

Following these " introductory pieces" were some of greater pretensions. One presenting the case of a gay young lady who had visited " Vanity Village," and returned with a head bewildered with " gallants, balls and sleigh-rides"—one calculated to repress superstition by its rehearsal of the experiences of Mrs. Goblin and Mrs. Tremor—one satirizing the boastfulness of farmers, and one intended to promote family discipline. Simple and harmless enough were these rural "theatricals," but doubtless answering their end. The next year the dramatic portion of the entertainment was given in the evening of the exhibition day, while arithmetic and spelling took the honors of the afternoon.

The date of this address is " Harwinton, October 14, 1802." The public exhibition appears, in this case, to have been given at the opening of the winter term.

In a valedictory address delivered to the " members of the Middle School District of Harwinton, in 1801," Mr. Humphrey discourses in more elevated strain upon the advantages of education in general. After specifying the ordinary motives which should influence the parent in providing the best possible education for his children, he refers to the recently acquired blessings of a free republic, and the jealous care with which it should be guarded. A part of this address glows with a true patriotic fervor, whose heats were always quickly kindled in his breast, if we may judge from a Fourth of July oration he delivered in Harwinton at about this period.

By the methods above described, the standard of public-school education was considerably raised. Improvement was made in every respect. Yet even then, "the three principal departments were spelling, reading and writing, with a smattering of geography and arithmetic." To carry the more advanced scholars a little farther, evening schools were often established.

As to Mr. Humphrey's own methods of government, they were eminently judicious for a period when the rod and the ferule were made so conspicuous in the armory of a school-house. Oliver Wendell Holmes is not the only man who counts it among the recollections of the school of his boyhood, that

"The tree that grew near it had the flavor of *birch*."

Mr. Humphrey had no code of laws. He simply required obedience and diligence of every pupil. He dealt in no threats, and although not insisting upon the abolition of the rod, never used it but once; although, he says quaintly, "I *shook* the mischief out of a good many."

"Wishing to keep alive an interest, through the summer, among the older scholars of the districts where I taught most, I used to write a sort of circular, and send it to them once in two or three months, urging them to keep up the habit of study as far as they were able, so as not to lose what they had gained. I also visited them, occasionally, by appointment; and I am quite sure that these little attentions were more to them than they cost me."

Of his "boarding 'round"—which expresses, in the vernacular, the prevalent custom of entertaining the teacher gratuitously in several families, a week, perhaps, being spent by him in each—he speaks approvingly, as useful both to himself and pupils, though he was always a visitor, and had never a home.

VIII.

H IS religious development began very early, in the home of his childhood. Neither of his parents was a professor of religion, in the technical sense, while he remained an inmate of their family. The theological teaching of the time was unfavorable to an early connection with the Church. The influence and the savor of Christianity were, however, always in the household where Mr. Humphrey was nurtured. His father and mother had both been trained in the atmosphere of Puritanism. Daily the father ministered at the family altar. All the outward observances of Christianity were rigidly enforced. The sunset of Saturday was the hither bound of " holy time." Then all work ceased, and all were enjoined to lay aside worldly cares, and compose themselves for the worship of the following day. Nor, although the Sabbath, as by Jewish rule, was supposed to end with Sunday's sunset, was any secular employment allowed on Sabbath evening. Even social visits were interdicted, that the impressions of the day might not be dissipated by talk and

3 *

laughter. The Sunday-school of modern times was then unknown; but the catechising of the afternoon made a Sunday-school of every family. Indeed, the Shorter Catechism was then taught in the public schools every Saturday morning; and the minister made it a part of his duty in pastoral visitation, to examine the children of his flock as to their familiarity with this universally adopted formulary of doctrine.

Mr. Humphrey was required, in his boyhood, to attend public worship with the strictest regularity. "I rarely stayed at home, whatever the weather might be, unless I was sick; which, in the good providence of God, was seldom the case. Once on a fast day, instead of going to meeting, I wandered over the fields and woods in the forenoon with a companion; but my conscience smote me so that I never tried it again."

It was not until the winter of 1798–9 that he had any marked religious experience. He was then in his twentieth year. Rev. Dr. Griffin, then settled at New Hartford, was preaching with all the freshness and ardor which characterized that remarkable man. A powerful revival began in his parish during the winter referred to. Its influences extended far and wide. They reached the parish where Mr. Humphrey resided. His heart and conscience were touched, but not until the revival had been some time in progress in Burlington. In his case "the process of awakening, inquiry, and conviction was very gradual." But he awoke at length to the consciousness that, although he desired to become a Christian, his "heart was opposed to God, to his government and his requirements." Once or twice before this, his thoughts had been seriously directed to the subject of personal holiness, under the faithful preaching of his pastor; but they had speedily been diverted. Now they abode with him day and night. He prayed; he read the Bible; he attended all the meetings; and as often as some friend expressed a personal hope in Christ, he murmured at the partiality of Him who "took one and another, while he was left." The rebellion of his heart became declared. "Were not some of these converts greater sinners than I? Have they sought salvation more diligently?" Then the doctrine of Divine Sovereignty, so earnestly insisted upon by the preachers of that day, presented itself to him in an odious light. "I saw it was in the Bible; I could not disprove it; yet I was very loth to believe it." He was not slow to use all the familiar arguments against it. "I took to myself the credit of entertaining more honorable thoughts of God's character and government than others; whilst, as I afterward

found, I was fighting against him. But God, of
his infinite mercy, was pleased to show me, after
I had struggled for weeks and months, that in his
electing love was all my hope. I became convinced
at length, that I never should repent if left to my
unassisted efforts. I was brought to feel that I lay
under the righteous condemnation of God's law, and
that he was under no obligation to save me. I
knew that salvation was freely offered through the
Atonement of Christ; I was urged to come to him
that I might have life; but I refused. I saw no
beauty in him that I should desire him. The invitation, 'Come, for all things are now ready,'
sounded continually in my ears; but I would not
come. It was my own fault; I could make nothing
else of it; but so obstinate and averse to holiness
was my heart, that I despaired of ever making myself better. If God did not give me a new heart I
must certainly perish. And here I saw that the
doctrine of election, which I had so stoutly opposed,
was my only ground of hope. It may be—this was
now my argument—that God, in the infinite riches
of his grace, has chosen me to salvation through
sanctification of the Spirit and belief of the truth.
If he has, he will make me willing in the day of
his power; for he never changes. His 'gifts and
calling are without repentance.' If there be no

election, I am lost; for I shall never come to Christ
'except the Father who hath sent him draw' me.
If I am not one of the elect according to the fore-
knowledge of God, woe is me for ever!

"This was my condition. This was the hope to
which I clung. I had too much light to expect to
enter the strait gate without striving; but I knew
that I should fail if the Saviour did not help me;
and my prayer was 'Lord, save, or I perish!' There
was no such marked and sudden change in my
feelings that I could ever, in looking back, fix upon
the day or week of my ' passing from death unto
life.' The light broke in gradually. It was some
time before I dared to indulge even a trembling
hope; and much longer before it was so confirmed
that I offered myself for admission into the Church."
He connected himself at last with the Congregational church in Burlington, Rev. Jonathan Miller,
pastor.

This record of experience is, perhaps, what one
would expect when considering the strong nature
of Mr. Humphrey and the presentations of truth to
which he was accustomed. Conversions are always
colored by prevailing ideas and habits of thought.
"If I was then born again," says he, " I was born
a *Calvinist*, ' Not of flesh nor of blood, nor of the
will of man, but of God, who hath mercy on whom

C

he will have mercy.' I then fully embraced the doctrines of the Shorter Catechism, and from this platform I have never swerved." Then follow some expressions of occasional doubt and fear, but closing with this: "Still *I cling to the cross*, I pray for strength and grace to fight the good fight of faith and lay hold on eternal life. Blessed Jesus, I cast myself upon thine Almighty arm, as one of the least and weakest of all saints, trusting alone in thine all-sufficient righteousness and atonement!" If the conflict with sovereignty was severe, the final dependence upon Christ was real and complete. There was both submission to God and faith in his dear Son. Under another form of preaching and habit of mind, the idea of Faith in Christ would have been most prominent. He would have been the "Calvinist" still. God was always great to him as a Sovereign, but Jesus always chief among ten thousand and altogether lovely.

He was himself accustomed to say, in later years, that the revivals and conversions of different periods are marked by peculiarities of type. But he always thought, as will hereafter appear, that, while in the earlier part of this century, the duty of immediate repentance was not sufficiently insisted upon, the "law-work," and the lengthened "concern" of the impenitent, sometimes continuing for many months,

resulted in a greater thoroughness of religious character than do the quicker experiences of the present
day. The converts of Dr. Griffin's time were certainly much better "indoctrinated" than those of
this period of faster, and, perhaps, more superficial,
movement.

IX.

THE clergymen to whose preaching Mr. Humphrey was early accustomed, were men of
genuine power, and of no inconsiderable culture.
He frequently heard others than his own pastor, as,
in the summer months, the necessities of agriculture,
to which all these clergymen were accustomed, took
the preacher away from his study and led to constant "exchanges." For many weeks the congregations expected to find strangers in their pulpits
every Sabbath. Mr. Miller was "a sound and instructive, but not eloquent preacher. His voice was
rather heavy than elastic; and though always serious, he rarely betrayed much emotion in the pulpit.
He was esteemed by his brethren in the Association
as one of their soundest theologians. As he lived
nearly a mile from the meeting-house, I remember
how he used always, in summer, to ride to meeting
on horseback—his wife on the pillion behind him.
After tying his horse in the shade he would walk in,

with his small Bible under his arm. The elderly part of the congregation, who ' sat below,' rose in a body as he passed up the aisle. When he had hung up his hat back of the pulpit, and turned round, the young people in the gallery all rose to receive his fatherly recognition."

Among the neighboring pastors were some of honored name—Rev. Jeremiah Hallock, of Canton; Rev. Giles Cowles, of Bristol; Rev. Dr. Griffin, already alluded to; Rev. Joseph Washburn, of Farmington; Rev. William Robinson, of Southington, described as being equal in metaphysical acumen and logical power to Dr. Dwight, of New Haven; Rev. Joshua Williams, of Harwinton, and Rev. Samuel J. Mills, of Torringford—a man noted for serious discourse, but also for many quaint flashes of humor.

These men were most faithful and laborious in their own parishes, through long-continued pastorates. Their missionary labors, also, were neither few nor small. They frequently went on journeys to the then distant and destitute regions of Vermont, where but few churches were gathered; and where the most of those which had begun to live were too feeble to support pastors. Thus this Connecticut Association furnished some germs for that handful of corn in the earth upon the top of the mountains, whose fruit now shakes like Lebanon—The American Home Missionary Society.

V.

AFTER reading this record of mental culture and religious experience, it does not surprise us that in the spring of 1803, Rev. Mr. Williams, of Harwinton, the clerical friend above alluded to, encouraged Mr. Humphrey to study with a view to the ministry. Nor are we surprised, that in view of the difficulties to be surmounted, even a man of resolute mind and consecrated heart, might, at first, shrink from such a path of duty. Mr. Humphrey was then in his twenty-fifth year. His Latin studies had extended no farther than "several books in Virgil and most of Cicero's Orations." It was now the month of May. Horace was to be read. Algebra was to be mastered. He had not even learned the alphabet of the Greek language, and must pass examination in the whole of the Greek Testament and in two books of Homer's Iliad. All this preparation must be made in six months. But after accustoming himself a little to the thought, Mr. Humphrey resolved to make the trial. Mr. Williams volunteered to conduct his recitations. He addressed himself to the task, and during those six

4

months applied himself to his studies twelve hours
each day. The Annual Commencement of Yale
College was then in September. Just before its
occurrence in this year, one of the professors—Rev.
Jeremiah Day, afterward President—spent a day or
two with Mr. Williams. He examined Mr. Humphrey sufficiently to give him encouragement to
present himself for admission to the Junior Class at
the close of the fall vacation. On the designated
day he appeared at the Institution.

" I had never been in New Haven before. Everything looked new and strange. My heart fluttered
when the hour of trial came. Two of the professors, Messrs. Day and Kingsley, examined me in
several branches of study. I was poorly fitted, as
they must have seen at a glance. I hardly did myself justice, perceiving which, perhaps, they made
some allowance, and admitted me, knowing my
anxiety for an education, and being willing to give
me a fair trial. I paid my fee of thirty dollars for
advanced standing, and brought my scanty furniture
into the room which was assigned me. This was a
new era in my life. It remained to be seen how I
could compete with classmates who had already
been accustomed to the drill of the recitation-room
for two years. My first trial was anything but satisfactory to myself. I was embarrassed. I often

blundered where I was sure I was prepared; but instead of relaxing my efforts under discouragement, I always resolved to do better next time. ·

" Taking an advanced standing, I was prepared for many difficulties, but encountered some which I did not expect. Though a Junior by the catalogue, I was really a *Freshman*. I had everything to learn of college customs, and of a hundred nameless things, before I could be wonted to my new life. When I entered Yale, the Junior and Senior Classes were allowed to send Freshmen on errands. The custom struck me as absurd. I never availed myself of it. I was glad that this privilege, together with that enjoyed by the Sophomores, was soon withdrawn."

Want of means occasioned another draft upon the strength and resolution of our student. He supplied the deficiency in part, at first, by acting as waiter in the dining-hall, where the students boarded " in commons." The custom was, to reduce the expense of boarding by a mutual association, the members of which used a kitchen and dining-room provided by the College, free of expense; nothing being charged for the food except the actual cost. A few of the students served as waiters for the rest, their compensation being afforded by a reduction of their bills for boarding. Such a service was considered no degradation, and affected in no way the social standing. During the third term of his Junior year, Mr. Humphrey became the bookkeeper of the establishment.

The custom was a bad one, notwithstanding its economy. Dr. Bushnell says that emigration tends to barbarism. College life, in the heart of cultivated society, was not without that tendency in those days. The dining-room of the " commons" was very long, and the students were hungry. To maintain some show of order, the College tutors sat at a table slightly elevated upon a platform at one end of the hall. One of them must always be in his place to crave a blessing at the commencement of the meal. The doors were kept locked until all was ready. Then the bell struck, and the whole mass of the besiegers, two or three hundred strong, rushed into the room. Each grasped his knife and fork, and stood ready for action as the last word of the " grace" was pronounced. Then came the racket and the struggle for the choicer viands. The platters were cleared in an instant. " Waiter! waiter!" resounded on every side. The unaccustomed visitor, respecting the ordinary decencies of the table, stood by in astonishment, and so lost his dinner. After a day or two, however, hunger overcame etiquette. So fierce was the general onset that " crockery" would have soon been annihilated. The table furniture was all of pewter. Even that was soon bored through by the forks of the invaders. Great pains was taken by the steward to furnish wholesome food, but he sometimes failed. Then, notwithstanding the presence and the watchful eyes of the tutors, scraps of butter and pieces of meat would fly, as if under the influence of invisible spirits, about the hall. Indignation meetings would sometimes be held; eloquent speeches would be made; a memorial, praying for a redress of grievances, would be sent to the president, though not always with much effect.

At the close of the Junior year, Mr. Humphrey found his finances running so low that he resorted to his old method of replenishing the treasury—the schoolmaster's work. This did not greatly interfere with his studies, as, during the Senior year, he had but one recitation per day, and that not difficult. He also discharged the duties of Librarian in one of the Society Halls; and thus was able to take his diploma without debt, and having a small sum with which to commence his professional studies.

In many respects his college life was very pleasant and profitable. He greatly enjoyed the sermons and lectures of President Dwight, whose eloquence in the class-room eclipsed even that of his pulpit

4 *

discourses. Jeremiah Day had then just been placed in the professorship of Mathematics and Natural Philosophy. Professor Silliman adorned the Laboratory, and Professor Kingsley was teacher of the Ancient Languages.

A powerful revival had brought large numbers of the students into the Church just before Mr. Humphrey entered college. His religious associations were therefore good.

His literary privileges, as member of the " Linonian," were greatly valued. He attended all the meetings of his society, and was always ready for debate, either as appointee, or as substitute for some lazier member. He was diligent also with his pen. He even courted the muses ; but, as he afterward thought, with indifferent success. His old taste for the work of the educator developed itself in several newspaper articles, published in one of the New Haven journals, over the signature *Lictor*. He used to thrust his manuscript under the door of the printing-office and hastily leave the premises. These articles attracted much attention ; but even the editor was ignorant of their authorship until after several of the series had been printed.

That the rank of our student in his class was by no means low, when the disadvantages under which he had labored are considered, is evidenced by the fact that his graduating appointment was an Oration. Among the well-known members of his class were that prominent educator of the blind, Rev. T. H. Gallaudet, and Rev. Dr. Spring, of New York.

After leaving college, Mr. Humphrey remained in New Haven a few months, in charge of a school; at the same time commencing his theological studies under the direction of President Dwight.

XI.

NO Theological Seminary then existed in the country. The " schools of the Prophets" were small, and scattered, mainly, in retired villages. Some pastor, well fitted for the task, would gather about him a few pupils each year, and instruct them as he was able. " In these private schools there was no critical study of the original languages of the Scriptures. The period of study, which rarely extended over eighteen months, was almost wholly occupied in reading standard English theological authors, such as Hopkins, Bellamy, and, above all, President Edwards; also in writing, and in disputations upon a long list of questions, embracing the whole system of Christian doctrine, drawn from the Word of God, and embodied in the Westminster Assembly's Catechism.

A favorite school of this class was conducted by Rev. Asahel Hooker, of Goshen, Connecticut. He was, in person, somewhat above medium stature, " well proportioned, of black hair, mild eye, sweet and placid countenance and lovely spirit. He had a clear mind; and, though not so profound as some of the great masters, was, on the whole, a good teacher. His preaching was sound, instructive and persuasive. It was eminently doctrinal, as well as highly practical and experimental. He was not an orator, but he had a good voice, which he managed well; and his delivery was winning in an uncommon degree."

Several of Mr. Humphrey's college acquaintances, already under the care of Mr. Hooker, invited him to join them. He did so in the spring of 1806, and became an inmate of Mr. Hooker's family. Four or five other students resided under the same hospitable roof which sheltered him. Some theological question was proposed for discussion at almost every meal. The ordinary debates were held in the class; dissertations were presented and subjected to the freest criticism. " We built an arbor during the following summer, in a beautiful primitive forest near by. There we used to declaim, and sometimes read, in pleasant weather. We exercised our voices in the meeting-house. We wrote three or four ser-

mons with which to begin our ministry. Still further
to prepare us for our work, Mr. Hooker took us with
him, or sent us to hold meetings in several districts
in his parish. He sent us every Sabbath, two and
two, to read sermons and conduct all the regular
services, excepting the benediction, in a remote
corner of the town, where a small meeting-house
had been built for ' winter privileges.' We selected
the best sermons we could find, and delivered. them
as well as we were able. By this means we were
gradually introduced to our work, so that when we
began to preach we felt the less embarrassment."

In October following, Mr. Humphrey was licensed
to preach by the Litchfield North Association, then
holding its sessions in Salisbury. He would gladly
have continued his studies, but yielded to the advice
of his friends and his own anxieties to be about his
Father's business. " With my license in my pocket,
I purchased a horse, saddle, bridle and portmanteau,
and was ready to enter the field, without knowing or
conjecturing in what corner of it I was to find employ. Up to this time my funds held out. I was
' even with the world,' paid all my bills, and had
a few dollars left—very few—for contingent expenses." He had " paid all the expenses of his
education without any aid, except that some of his
clothes had been furnished by his mother."

He preached his first sermon in the pulpit of Rev. Mr. Stone, at Cornwall, Connecticut, and before a meeting of ministers. The following Sabbath, he preached at Watertown, in the absence of the pastor of that village. A week or two subsequently, he received an invitation to preach as candidate at Fairfield. He went to that place early in November, having but four or five sermons; and preached "straight on" three months, and then went away. Very soon after he left, he received a unanimous call from the church and society of Fairfield, to become their pastor. While considering this call, he preached in his old haunt, "the winter privileged" meeting-house of Goshen. He then returned to Fairfield.

XII.

THIS town is pleasantly situated on Long Island Sound, twenty miles west of New Haven. It was then "a considerable village, and the half-shire town of the county; but very plain in its external appearance. Not more than four or five of the houses, I believe, had ever been painted, and these were now so weatherbeaten that the signs of paint had wellnigh disappeared. Fairfield had been burnt, during the Revolution, by that bloody traitor Arnold. By this calamity the inhabitants were very much impoverished, and were obliged to rebuild in as plain a style as was consistent with the comfort of their families."

He found an uncommon social equality in the village. "Some had more property and intelligence than others; but while none were rich, few were very poor. And there was a freedom and cordiality in social intercourse which was delightful. Whole neighborhoods lived together like one great family of many branches." This was attributed to the fellowship of suffering, produced by the calamities of war. "There was at that time very little enterprise in Fairfield. The farmers maintained their families comfortably, but their sons generally left them for more inviting and lucrative fields, as soon as they had reached their majority. Many went into the coasting trade; others into the cities, where some became rich and then retired upon their fortunes. But although Fairfield was a social, friendly and moral place, it was not, strictly speaking, religious. The church was small, the rules of admitting members were very lax, and discipline was greatly neglected. Upon inquiry, I could find but two members of the church who prayed daily with their families. Two or three others, I believe not more, prayed on the Sabbath and sometimes on week-days. When I settled there, not a man could I call upon to lead in prayer at a religious meeting. Not one had ever prayed in public. Nothing like a revival in the congregation was remembered by any one. Doubtless there had been many conversions. There had been no revival." The congregation had never been long without a pastor; but when he was absent —as he generally was each summer—sometimes for weeks together, the meeting-house was never opened. Such a thing as a deacon's meeting was unknown to them.

" This condition of affairs was largely due to the prevalence of the ' Half-way Covenant,' which was then quite a feature of church-life in New England. This was an expedient adopted to secure the baptism of infants whose parents had never made public profession of religion. The conditions of the ' Half-way Covenant' were, that parents who desired baptism for their children, must, before presenting them for the ordinance, ' give their assent to certain Church articles, expressing a belief in the Bible as the Word of God,' engaging to lead a good moral life, to bring up their children in a religious way, and to come to the Lord's Table, or into full communion, as soon as they should see their way clear." This gave church membership to those who made no pretensions to personal holiness, and admitted them to the Lord's Table without piety. The " way" to

the table was "seen clear," in general, at some period
of unusual seriousness, like that of affliction. The
custom thus established was afterward continued.
Some were perhaps genuine converts; but very
many were not. As a consequence of this system,
a regular Church membership, formed after the
usual method, was very rare. "A lady, then eighty
years of age, born in Fairfield, and always a resident, told me she had never known but one young
person, whom she named, to join the church."
Doctrinal preaching also had been very much neglected. Formalism and morality had extensively
taken the place of true devotion and godliness.

These facts coming to Mr. Humphrey's knowledge while he was preaching at Fairfield, before
his call to the pastorate, he aimed to be explicit in
the statement of his views. He preached the strong
doctrines of that Calvinism in which he had been
trained, and into which he had been converted. "I
told the people that I could find no warrant in Scripture for this 'Half-way Covenant,' and that in no
case could I administer the ordinance of baptism to
children, neither of whose parents was in full communion with the Church." It seemed to him very
unlikely that such "trial sermons" as these would
result in a call. But the way had been somewhat
prepared for them by the previous faithful preaching

of Rev. Noah Porter, afterward his brother-in-law, who had supplied the pulpit for a short period, but was now settled in Farmington.

Nevertheless, the call came, as we have seen. It was accepted, and the day of ordination was fixed. The events immediately following are thus described by Rev. William B. Sprague, D.D., in a communication to the *New York Observer:*

"When he returned to them after having accepted their call, he called on Mrs. Eliot, his predecessor's widow, and asked her to show him the Confession of Faith and Covenant which were in use in the Church. She brought to him a little piece of paper, containing, as a Confession of Faith, little more than a recognition of the divine authority of the Scriptures, while the Covenant was something like this : ' We promise to devote our children to God in baptism, and when we see our own way clear, to come also to the Holy Communion.' He immediately called on Judge Sturges, one of the most prominent members of the church, and asked him if that formed the whole basis of communion in their church; and he told him that it did. Mr. Humphrey then told the Judge, with all frankness, that he could not settle on such a basis; but the Judge advised him not to make any trouble about it, and intimated that it would be easy to remedy the difficulty afterward. Mr. H. insisted that, if it were not remedied at once, he should feel constrained to withdraw his acceptance of the call. 'What, then,' said the Judge, 'shall be done?' Said Mr. Humphrey: 'I will draw up a Confession of Faith, and do you draw up one also, and let us see how far they agree.' And to this the Judge consented. Mr. Humphrey prepared one embracing all the leading orthodox doctrines; but when he asked the Judge for his, it turned out that he had only written an article or two, which, however, suited Mr. Humphrey so well, that he willingly incorporated them with those he had written himself.

"A church meeting was now called to see whether they would adopt the new ecclesiastical basis; but, in the mean time, it had come to be noised abroad that there was trouble arising, and that it was doubtful whether the ordination would take place. Mr. Humphrey was quite as popular with the congregation as with the church; and they manifested a deep interest in the result of the church meeting. There was a very general attendance of the members; and when they had assembled, Mr. Humphrey read the old articles and made his objections to them; and then the new ones, and gave his reasons in their favor. The church was then called upon to express their opinion, and the result was the

unanimous adoption of the new articles. The way
was now clear for the ordination. But the question
arose, after the ordination, how the ' Half-way Covenant' folks should be disposed of. The church
voted that all who had owned the Covenant, and
were not in full communion, should have six months
to consider whether they should come to the ordinance of the Supper or not; and that, in case they
decided in favor of coming, nothing more should be
necessary than that they should signify their wish to
the pastor—otherwise they would be considered as
not belonging to the church. Some came, and
some who did not within that time, were afterward
hopefully converted. About a year after his settlement, Roger Minot Sherman moved into Fairfield,
and was ever afterward an important helper to him
in his ministry."

XIII.

MR. HUMPHREY was ordained March 16,
1807, Rev. Mr. Miller, his former pastor,
preaching the sermon. His ministry in Fairfield
continued about ten years.

He felt it to be his duty, immediately after his
ordination, to establish a weekly prayer-meeting;
but as no member of his church was willing to lead
in public devotion, he began by privately collecting

a few of the more pious and gifted of the members, agreeing with them that each person of the little circle should lead in prayer at each of their informal meetings. In this way a few of them gradually gained sufficient confidence to assist in public meetings.

The discipline of the church was also restored. "Cases were taken up and disposed of very harmoniously. There seemed to be a common desire to purge out the old leaven, and to keep the unity of the Spirit in the bonds of peace."

In forming his plans of labor, he resolved to preach two carefully-prepared sermons in the meeting-house each Sabbath, and to deliver an extempore lecture each week in one of the "out-districts" of the town, taking the districts in rotation. This method he found very satisfactory, as affording his people and himself the benefit of both the more elaborate and the freer discourse.

His pastoral visitations were also, after the first three or four years, systematized; public notice being given from the pulpit, each Sabbath, of the district he would visit in the ensuing week; the very day when he might be expected by any particular family being specified. By this method he generally reached all the members of his parish, and held religious services with all the families of his

5 *

flock, as he went "preaching and teaching from house to house."

These methods appear to have been fruitful in promoting the spiritual life of the church and the conversion of souls. There was, however, for some time, no revival. Mr. Humphrey and his more earnest parishioners mourned and prayed over "the desolations of Zion." "Our prayer was in public and in private, 'O Lord, revive thy work.' And we were not alone. The Association to which I belonged was led to the inquiry, 'Lord, what wilt thou have us to do?' A monthly concert of prayer for the outpouring of the Spirit was agreed upon. The pastors went forth, 'two and two,' upon a visit to all the parishes of the district. The report at the next meeting of the Association was discouraging. In most places the concert was thinly attended. There was nowhere a noise or shaking among the dry bones. The question went round—Shall the concert be continued another year? The vote was unanimous in the affirmative. The year wore away like the preceding, without any special token of the Divine presence : our faith was again put to the test. Should the concert be continued? No one was ready to give it up. We agreed to make more special efforts to rouse the minds of Christians in our several parishes. This condition prevailed for

three or four years. We were ready to ask in our
despondency, 'Are the mercies of God clean gone
for ever?' 'Will he be favorable no more?' At
length the set time came, and the heavens poured
down righteousness. Eleven of our seventeen parishes shared more or less in the blessing. Our
mourning was turned to rejoicing, and we were
ready to say, one to another, 'What hath God
wrought! Lo, this is our God. We have waited
for him and he will save us; this is the Lord; we
have waited for him; we will be glad and rejoice in
his salvation!'"

In Fairfield the revival began suddenly in the
Academy, the pupils of which were mostly under
fourteen years of age. It soon extended throughout
the parish. "It was a new thing in Fairfield, and
'marvelous in their eyes.' The church was very
much strengthened, and the revival changed the
face of things in many of our leading families."
Owing to the peculiar conditions which had so long
existed in the congregation, and in accordance with
the practice of the day, none of the converts were
admitted into the church until after a 'probation' of
several months. Every human test of conversion
was applied, and the younger converts were long
subjected to catechetical instruction.

Who, while reading the history of this revival,

can fail to think of Elijah upon Carmel, praying,
and then sending his servant to the outlook, that he
might scan the brazen horizon as it bent to the
cloudless sea—praying and looking for the cloud
seven times before the first indication of rain was
seen? Also, how, when at last the cloud rose upon
the west, it spread like magic over the sky, and
broke in torrents upon the thirsty land?

XIV.

A S may be surmised from the course of this nar-
rative, Mr. Humphrey was always ready to
identify himself with any public movement which
promised to benefit society at large. He had not
been long settled at Fairfield before the "Moral Society of Connecticut" was formed. The object of this
society was to secure a better observance of the Sabbath, and, if possible, to check the tide of intemperance which was sweeping over the land. Whatever
would promote good morals appears also to have
been included in the plan of the organization. A
similar society existed in Yale College while Mr.
Humphrey was a student in that institution. We find
among his college papers an " Oration on Account-
ability to God," which he delivered in 1804, in the
early part, probably, of his Senior year, before a

meeting of that society. Its introduction is as
follows :—

" To unite all the serious and well-disposed members of Yale College in the bonds of harmony and
friendship, to promote the cause of true morality,
and to check the alarming progress of vice, were
the objects for which the Moral Society was insti-
tuted. Whatever, therefore, has a tendency to accomplish these important objects, cannot fail of
being deeply interesting to every individual present.
And as a solemn and realizing sense of accountabil-
ity to God is so material here, and is a subject which
so nearly concerns us all, I shall make no apology
for introducing it on the present occasion."

Of the Temperance movement in this country,
Mr. Humphrey was one of the earliest and most
vigorous pioneers. In the winter of 1811–12, he
preached several sermons on this subject to his congregation. It was a delicate subject, for very many
of the families in his congregation made daily use
of intoxicating drinks. He assailed the evil, however, with his wonted fearlessness. The convictions
which began in the harvest-field, when, as a matur-
ing boy, he found that he could accomplish more
without the aid of spirituous fluids than with it,
were confirmed by the experience and the observations of the man. Two of the sermons alluded to

are before us. The first of them—a " double-ser-
mon"—is founded upon Prov. xx. 1 : " Wine is a
mocker: strong drink is raging." The materials
upon which he depended for facts and principles
were scanty. " I had not then seen anything to aid
me except a small pamphlet by Dr. Rush, of Philadelphia." But he made good use of his materials.

" I am aware"—so runs the sermon, after its introduction has brought out the necessities of the case
—" that almost every step of my progress will be
on tender ground. It is a melancholy fact that
most, if not all, even of our religious assemblies
contain some who are themselves addicted to excess-
ive drinking. And where this is not the case—if
indeed such a congregation can be found—many
who compose it have friends that are deeply involved in the guilt and shame of this worse than
brutal practice. For these reasons it is difficult,
perhaps impossible, to avoid the appearance and
suspicion of personalities in preaching against it.
Besides, I will frankly tell you, my hearers, that in
the course I deem it my duty to pursue, I hope to
suggest something profitable for admonition, for re-
proof and instruction, to the most pious and temperate part of my congregation. While, on the
one hand, I solemnly disclaim any intention unne-
cessarily to wound the feelings of those who hear

me. I will not knowingly ' daub with untempered mortar.' It is a case of life and death. The evils of intemperate drinking must be faithfully pointed out. Those who have begun to go after the monster must be pulled back with friendly violence. The innocent and inexperienced must be warned."

Then follows an exposition of the text :

" Wine is a mocker. It makes fools of those who use it to excess. Then they are prepared to scoff at the conscientious, and treat even things sacred with mockery. Strong drink is raging. It gives its victims no rest. It creates an appetite which nothing can satisfy. It rages like a fever in the body, like a demon in the head, like a wild beast in the family, like a pestilence in the community."

We have no space for the glowing arguments which follow. They have since become familiar in the literature of this reformation. One leaf we give from his own observation :

" I have seen the fires of genius extinguished by strong drink. I have known men who once were numbered with the wise and honorable, gradually reduced almost to a level with idiots by intemperance. I have seen the masculine and discriminating mind dwindling into premature old age and second childhood. I have known of more than one promising youth, tender and well beloved, of high hopes and of flattering prospects, ensnared and taken by the subtle enemy. The doting parent began to tremble and weep over his son. Hope and comfort fled from the abode of him who begat and of her who bore him. The young man who had begun to attract the attention and to gain the confidence of the public, neglected the culture of his mind, benumbed all his faculties by excess, and sank away into insignificance and contempt. When I extend my view, and think how many thousands of minds have been destroyed in the same way, it reminds me of some noble city in ruins. I walk over the spot where it stood, examine with painful reflections the fallen columns and broken arches, survey the broad foundations of magnificent buildings which are no more, and sigh to think the glory is departed for ever."

The double-shotted sermon of the following Sunday was upon the text, "Look not upon the wine when it is red," etc., Prov. xxiii. 31, 32. In this he considers "The causes and the insidious progress of Intemperance." Wine-bibbers received no more comfort from this discourse than did the devotees of distilled liquor from the first. "It is the bad pre-eminence of the rich and the great to ruin their health, drown their reason, extinguish their natural affections and murder their souls with wine. It is a happy circumstance, that, with us, the common people cannot afford to share in this expensive kind of intemperance. When, however, I say that excess in wine is mostly confined to the rich and the great, I mean nothing more than that many such are addicted to it. Can this qualified charge be denied? . . . . If we could know the whole truth, how many bankruptcies are produced by this expensive mode of sinning against God and of plunging both soul and body into hell! How many creditors are defrauded, how many families are beggared, how many hearts are broken!"

The ground of this sermon was really that of Total Abstinence—a ground not generally taken by the most of the advocates of temperance up to that day.

The fervid words thus spoken in Fairfield were not without effect. They were reiterated in other places. The subject was brought before the Fairfield West Association, with which Mr. Humphrey and his church were connected. Resolutions were adopted, by which the use of ardent spirits was interdicted at meetings of the Association, and pledges were made to discourage, by conversation and by example, both the use and the vending of spirituous liquors. Mr. Humphrey was appointed chairman of a committee to prepare an address to the churches

6

on the subject.   This address was full of the arguments and appeals which had been presented in the
pulpit at Fairfield It was widely circulated, and
produced a marked result.

" The reports of ministers and delegates at the
next annual meeting were exceedingly encouraging.
It appeared that a great change had been produced
in the views and habits of all the more enlightened
classes throughout the district.   In some churches
and congregations the consumption of ardent spirits
had been reduced one-third, in others, one-half, and
in others, more than half.   In nearly all the respectable
families within our limits, the decanters and glasses
had been swept from the sideboards ; a great many
of our church members and others had adopted the
principle of *total abstinence;* some of our largest
farmers carried the principle successfully through
haying and harvesting ; all our ministers had entered
heartily into the reformation ; and I am confident
that from that day to this, embracing a period of
twenty-two years, no ardent spirit has been provided
at their stated meetings."

No more consistent advocate of these principles
has ever been found than was Mr. Humphrey to
the close of his career.

In 1815, he preached a sermon before the
Connecticut Moral Society, at New Haven, which

was printed, and is full of impulse and encouragement.

XV.

ON the 20th of April, 1808, one year after his settlement in Fairfield, Mr. Humphrey was married to Sophia Porter, only daughter of Deacon Noah Porter, of Farmington. A fitting tribute to her memory, by one of her sons-in-law, may be found at the close of this volume. In the autobiographical sketches occurs a reference to this event, which is full of devout thankfulness to that God who provided such an "help meet for him." No wife was ever loved more truly; no husband was ever more honored. No children ever more revered a mother before whom it was a delight to rise up and call her blessed, than did her offspring.

XVI.

THE ten years of life in Fairfield wore swiftly and happily away. The causes which led to a severance of the pastoral relation at the end of this period were these :

The salary of six hundred dollars, which was at first sufficient, became inadequate for the support of a growing family. The war of 1812 occasioned a rapid advance in the prices of the necessaries of

life. The first expedient for supplying deficiencies
was, to receive a few boys, pupils in the Academy,
into the family as boarders. But this expedient told
severely upon the health of Mrs. Humphrey, never,
in that portion of her life, very strong. Many a
night she sat at her table, repairing the raiment of
her boarders, until the " wee sma' hours ayant the
twal," only to rise before the dawn to superintend
the preparation of their meals; her "help" being of
the most unreliable sort.

The health of Mr. Humphrey also yielded under
the pressure of his labors. His eyes, in consequence of what he terms injudicious habits of study,
suddenly failed. For several months he was unable
to use them in reading, writing or preaching.
When at length he began to recover their use, he
employed an amanueusis; and the fair, round cha-
racters of his wife's penmanship were often found in
his manuscripts. We have one sermon before us,
prepared at this period, in which his own chirogra-
phy alternates curiously with that of his assistant.
Some difficulty in the way of increasing the salary
was also experienced, partly from the indifference
of a few who still clung to their prejudices in respect
of the Half-way Covenant. It gradually became
evident that the pastoral tie must be broken. In
1816, the vacant pulpit of Middletown was virtually

offered him. It was the pulpit which, of all others
in Connecticut, he would have preferred; but at that
time the fruits of the revival we have described were
ungathered. He could not then leave his harvest-
field. The year passed; the harvest was over. He
announced his intention to request a dismission.
Amid many remonstrances a meeting of the Consociation was called, and " after a full hearing," yet in
the face of many protests, both from the church and
the members of the Consociation, he was dismissed,
May, 1817.

XVII.

LEAVING his family in Fairfield, he preached a
few Sabbaths in Hartford. While there he
received an urgent invitation to visit a vacant Congregational church in Pittsfield, Massachusetts. He
complied with the invitation. He found the church
in a somewhat critical condition. Two divided portions of one " tribe" were seeking reunion. A few
years previous a political convulsion had rent the
church. One party withdrew, built a new meeting-
house and settled a minister, Rev. Mr. Punderson.
" The other party retained their aged pastor, and,
after his death, settled his son, Rev. Mr. Allen.
There was for some time great bitterness of feeling
on both sides; but it gradually subsided, and at the

6 *   E

end of seven years there was found to be a strong
and general disposition to reunite. There was no
need of two congregations. One minister could
care for all." Some opposed reunion, but both
pastors favored it. To promote it, both resigned,
and the two congregations came together under the
old roof. The difficult process of organic reunion
was now to be promoted. Mr. Humphrey was soon
invited to undertake the task. He shrank from it.
He feared the effect of the severe climate of the
Berkshire hills upon his family. His "politics"
might be regarded with suspicion. But some one
must become their pastor. "I did not wish to go to
Pittsfield. Not that I had any objection to the people. They were an intelligent congregation. There
was a good degree of active piety in the church,
and they had treated me kindly. But the congregation was spread over the whole town—six miles
square. They were united, but not amalgamated.
A good deal of the old leaven remained. Some of
the prominent families stood aloof. And, to increase
my perplexity, I was strongly solicited to return and
be resettled over the church and congregation in
Fairfield. I was assured of a competent support.
But my convictions of duty at length overcame my
objections. I became convinced that the ' call' was
from a higher source than the voice of the people,

and that it was not for me to *choose*, but to *obey*. I accepted the call, and was installed in November, 1817, by a council." Rev. Dr. Hyde, of Lee, preached the installation sermon.

The call reveals the transition then taking place from the old parish system to that of modern times. By the then existing laws of Massachusetts, the whole population of each town was taxable for the support of the pastor, except such as filed certificates setting forth that they belonged to some other than the Congregational denomination. Thus the settlement of a pastor was a "town-meeting affair." Certain lands for the use of the pastor were set apart by the township, and the salary was thus provided for by a sort of Puritanic union of Church and State.

Mr. Humphrey's call is in these words:

"At a legal meeting of the freeholders and other inhabitants of the town of Pittsfield, belonging to the Congregational Society in said town, qualified by law to vote in town affairs, at the Town-House in said town, on Monday the 15th day of September, 1817,

"*Voted*, That Joshua Danforth be moderator.

"*Voted*, That the town agree to unite with the Church of the Congregational Society, in inviting the Rev. Mr. Humphrey to settle over them in the

Gospel ministry: provided an agreement can be made with him for his salary agreeable to the views of the town.

"*Voted*, That in case the Rev. Heman Humphrey shall conclude to accept the invitation of the town to settle over them in the work of the Gospel ministry, they will, and do, hereby agree to grant him the sum of nine hundred dollars as his stated salary, so long as he shall continue their minister as aforesaid: provided that he shall relinquish to the town all claims that he may have to the ministry lands or property belonging to the town.

"*Voted*, That Josiah Bissell, Esq., Gen. John B. Root, Mr. Samuel D. Colt and Nathan Willis, Esq., be a committee to convey the invitation to Rev. Heman Humphrey, of Fairfield, Connecticut, to settle over the Congregational Church and Society in this town, in the work of the Gospel ministry; and who are also authorized to offer him the sum of $900 as his annual stated salary, on the conditions stated in the preceding vote."

When Mr. Humphrey was installed the whole town virtually formed his parish. A feeble Baptist church existed in the western portion of the township; a few Methodists were scattered here and there, but enjoyed no regular preaching. Some families neglected the Sanctuary; but with the ex-

ceptions noted, all were under his pastoral care,
whether they attended public worship or not.

Pittsfield is one of the most beautiful towns in
Massachusetts. It occupies a high plateau, en-
circled by the lower ranges of the Green Mountains. The whole horizon is rimmed by hills. On
the east is the range from which the Ashley pours
its arterial streams for the water-supply of the
village. On the west is a somewhat irregular
range, from the crown of which one may see the
valley of the peaceful Hudson spreading its emerald
floor to the base of the Catskills. On the north the
blue summits of Saddle Mountain close in the
view. The southern horizon is pierced by the valley of the Housatonic. Nearly all the hills are partially shorn of their forests. Rich pasture-lands
creep up the slopes, and appear to end in sharp but
softened lines against the sky. Four beautiful lakes
present their mirrors to the passing clouds and to
the fringes of foliage on their shores. The atmosphere is famed for its purity, and for the brilliancy
of the effects of sunlight and shadow produced in
summer days. Nowhere are sunsets more beautiful; nowhere are beautiful sunsets more frequent.
The western hills are distant enough for long per-
spectives of evening cloud; they are near enough
to catch all the glories of the departing light. They

often appear as if transfigured, in their dreamy mists of mingled rose and gold.

When Mr. Humphrey was installed, the village consisted of four streets, broad and shaded, meeting at a small park in the centre. The names of these streets were derived from the four points of the compass toward which they led. At the focus of the village, in the centre of the park, stood a forest elm, which unfolded its leafy canopy from the summit of a tall and shapely trunk. This elm was long the pride of the town, and was preserved with jealous care for many years after age and storm had deprived it of its beauty. It was not removed until decay had so weakened it that it creaked and threatened to fall in every unusual wind. When at last it was removed in consideration of public safety, the inhabitants gathered sadly to see it fall. Twigs and leaves, as well as branches, were borne away as mementoes. The sounder portions of the huge trunk were cut and shaped into little articles to be preserved by children's children.

Directly opposite this elm stood the meeting-house of the Congregational church—a large and well finished structure of wood. It has now given place to a more enduring edifice of stone, in the tower of which the clock, presented by a wealthy citizen in 1823, still marks the hours. Mr. Humphrey's resi-

dence was on East street, in a house since owned
by the Campbell family. It has been greatly
altered; but the magnificent maples, many of
which were planted by Mr. Humphrey, still stand
before it.

When he assumed the charge of the congregation, "very few of its leading men, such as law-
yers, physicians and merchants, were professors of
religion." They were, however, regular attendants
of public worship. The first object of the new pastor was to win the respect of all for the pulpit.
But little pastoral visiting was, therefore, attempted
during the first winter. The effects of careful study
being realized, systematic visitation began in the
opening spring, and was vigorously conducted
through the succeeding months. The old methods
so successful in Fairfield were adopted. A weekly
lecture was established in the out-districts. The
Sunday-school, which then began to take a recognized place among the institutions of the Church,
received much attention. The baptized children of
the church were collected once in three months, for
public catechetical instruction. A Bible-class of
young women was also established. Soon all was
working smoothly, and success crowned every form
of pastoral labor. Old wounds began to heal, and
the congregation gradually became organically one.

Many anecdotes of Mr. Humphrey's skill and prudence in winning the disaffected or the indifferent are still related by his parishioners. One of those oftenest repeated is that of his conquering the heart of a farmer who had steadily refused to attend the Sabbath services. By visiting him in his harvest-field, and, without a word of professional exhortation, engaging him in conversation upon farming, and then taking his "cradle," cutting a swath of grain, as if he had been used only to a farmer's life all his days.

His educational tastes also had free exercise in the schools of the town, which he regularly visited as a member of the school-committee. These visits gave him great influence, particularly over the children of the parish.

XVIII.

THE principal event of his ministry in Pittsfield was a remarkable revival, whose history has been perpetuated as prominent in the movements of Rev. Dr. Nettleton's day. Up to 1820, no general revival had ever been known in the town. In the spring of that year, revivals began to occur in some of the neighboring villages. The church in Pittsfield was roused to unusual prayer. On the first Sabbath in May the sacrament of the Lord's Supper was celebrated with unusual solemnity. Immediately afterward, the early rain appeared. An interesting journal kept by the pastor, records the history of several succeeding weeks.

About forty, most of whom were received into the church in the autumn, were the fruits of this summer's awakening.

In May following, Rev. Asahel Nettleton, the evangelist, came to visit Mr. Humphrey, for the purpose of rest from his exhausting labors. A general desire to hear him was immediately expressed. He did not yield to it at first; but being persuaded to deliver an evening lecture, he saw such signs of encouragement that his rest was soon at an end. "In two or three weeks we had unmistakable evidence that God had again begun to revive his work. Our lecture-room was crowded; men were there who had not been wont to attend our evening meetings, and there was a very marked solemnity in the congregation on the Sabbath. Through the whole month of June the interest increased among all classes; toward the close, very rapidly. By the middle of July the work was at its height. It pervaded all classes, and extended to all parts of the town; but principally affected heads of families, particularly the prominent men of the village. The whole face of the community was changed. Re-

7

ligion was the all-absorbing topic of conversation.
The revival continued all summer. On the first
Sabbath of November the harvest was gathered in;
and a glorious harvest it was. Between eighty and
ninety, the rich and the poor, the high and the low,
stood up together in the long, broad aisle, and before
angels and men, avouched the Lord to be their God,
and were received into the church. Never had such
a scene been witnessed in Pittsfield. The joy of the
church overflowed in tears and thanksgivings. I am
sure there must have been great joy in heaven."

Many of the incidents of this revival are of unusual interest. We record but one, perhaps the most
striking of all. On the Fourth of July, the religious
interest was so absorbing that it was determined to
substitute for the usual noisy celebration of the day,
a service with sermon in the meeting-house. Mr.
Humphrey was designated to preach the sermon.
The meeting was appointed to be held at two o'clock
P. M. As, however, he was busy on the morning
of the Fourth in preparing his discourse, he was
waited upon by a committee of young men, who
informed him that they had arranged for an *oration*
of the usual sort, to be delivered in the forenoon, in
the meeting-house. He was desired to " open the
meeting with prayer." These young men had been
incited to this act of opposition by some of the ene-

mies of the revival, in the village. The usual " In-
dependence dinner" was also to be held in a public
hall near the church. Mr. Humphrey declined the
invitation of the committee; but the oration was
delivered.

The hour for the religious service arrived, and the
house was filled with a solemn and reverent congregation. The young men and their companions of
the morning assembly gathered in the park in front
of the church, and amused themselves with fire-
crackers, etc., as the service went on. The hour
for the public dinner approached. Toasts were to
be drunk, according to the usual custom, to the
firing of cannon in the park. A promise had been
made that all such noisy demonstrations should be
deferred until the close of the religious services.
But as the sermon was protracted, the celebrators on
the green became impatient. They procured a drum
and fife, and marched beneath the windows of the
meeting-house. A few of the congregation went
quietly out to silence the noise, but poorly succeeded. The service within went on 'amidst the
disturbance. The " patriotic" crowd resolved to try
the effect of gunpowder, and applied the match to
their cannon.

" The first discharge shook the house. My text
was, '*If the Son make you free, ye shall be free*

indeed.' It was one of the most appropriate I could think of for the occasion. In two or three minutes there was another discharge. The shock of the first being over, the second produced a solemnity more profound than the sermon would have occasioned, and gave me opportunity for enlargement which I had not anticipated. I had reached the application of my sermon. By the time of the third discharge the whole congregation seemed perfectly composed. As the cannonading went on, I took occasion to hold up the contrast between Christ's freemen and the servants of Satan, as strikingly illustrated both without and within the house. By this train of extempore remark I added something like a quarter of an hour to the length of the sermon. Each discharge of the cannon overpowered my voice for a moment, but I went on. When I had finished, I called upon Rev. Dr. Shepherd, of Lenox, who was present, to lead in prayer. His remarkably heavy voice sounded triumphantly over the disturbance. When we came out, some of our more prominent men, among whom was the sheriff of the county, were very much excited, and proposed to have the leading rioters arrested and punished. I said, ' By no means. In attacking us they have shot themselves through and through. They have so outraged the feelings of the whole community that we have only to leave them to themselves, and go on with our Master's work, praying God to give them repentance.'

"I have never witnessed a more striking example of the moral sublime than on that day and evening. Those who had been foremost in the disturbance hastened away as soon as they could. By eight o'clock there was scarcely a soul left upon the green; whereas, on all former like occasions, a large number lingered there and kept up their ' celebration' until late at night. The evening lecture, which had been appointed from the desk under the cannon's roar, was unusually full and solemn. The work went on for some days with more power than ever. We had but to ' stand still and see the salvation of the Lord.'"

A writer in the *Charleston* (S. C.) *Intelligencer*, describing this scene, says:

" So skillfully did the preacher allude to and apply his discourse to the conduct of the opposition out of doors; such advantage did he take of every blast of the cannon and every play of the drum, by some well-pointed remark, that it all went like a two-edged sword to the hearts of listening sinners. Indeed Mr. H. afterward informed me, that had he showed the heads of his sermon to his opposers previously, and earnestly requested them, when he

7*

reached such a point in his sermon to *fire*, and when he reached another point to *fire*, they could not more effectually have subserved the purpose of his discourse than they did. Those gentlemen who had walked in the opposers' procession, hung their heads, were disgusted, and in some instances were convicted deeply of sin. One gentleman who had been previously somewhat serious, declared to me that every shot of the cannon pierced his soul, filled him with an indescribable horror, and brought him, through the blessing of God, to such a hatred and detestation of sin in himself and others, as constrained him quickly to fly to Christ.

"I sat near the Rev. Mr. Nettleton; and so delighted was he with the discourse, and so accurately *prescient*, too, was he of the result, that whenever an apt allusion dropped from the lips of the preacher, he would turn round with a holy smile; and whenever a shot from the cannon pierced our ears he would say—it would involuntarily escape from him—' *That is good—that is good.*' Speaking afterward of the events of this day he observed to me: ' Did you not feel calm? I thought there was a deep majestic calm overspreading the minds of Christians.'"

Great care was taken in the instruction of the converts of this revival; and they, with their children, have been among the most honored members of the church to the present day.

The experience thus obtained confirmed in Mr. Humphrey's heart a love for revivals which he never lost. Few have been more judicious and successful in promoting and conducting them than he. He was often invited to aid his brother pastors in their revival labors. In the winter of 1822 he was especially active in assisting Rev. Sereno Dwight, of the Park Street Church, Boston. He was always a firm friend of Dr. Nettleton; and, when occasion required, his staunch defender.

XIX.

IN 1823, Mr. Humphrey received the degree of Doctor of Divinity from Middlebury College. He had at this time before him an invitation to assume the Presidency of the Collegiate Institution which now bears the name of Amherst College. Rev. Dr. Moore, the first President, died in June, 1823. In July, Dr. Humphrey was elected to the vacant position. He describes this appointment as occasioning "the most trying crisis of my pastoral life."

He was ardently attached to his people. They were equally attached to him. To go, was to leave the pastoral office in one of the largest and most desirable congregations of the State. As pastor he was eminently successful; could he hope to be equally successful as President? The Institution to which he was invited had no permanent foundation, except in the hearts and the prayers of its friends. A petition for a college charter had the year before been unceremoniously thrown out of the Legislature of the State, nearly all the representatives, including those from Amherst itself, voting against it. Yet he could not dismiss the invitation without a thought. His parishioners, when they learned that the invitation had been extended, smiled; when they learned that he was considering it, they remonstrated; when he proposed a council of his brethren to aid him in deciding the question of duty, they declined. He was obliged to call a council without their co-operation. That council advised him to accept the Presidency. The congregation most reluctantly consented, and the pastoral bond was dissolved. "Nothing now remained but to make arrangements for my removal, and to take those sad farewells, which cost me more anguish of soul than anything in my long life, except the loss of children." These farewells over, he removed to Amherst, and was inducted into office, October 15, 1823.

XX.

AMHERST is scarcely less beautiful as a village than Pittsfield. Its horizons are wider, and their outlines are less bold. Standing upon the tower of the college chapel, one's eye follows the regular line of the parapet of the eastern hills, till, bending around to the south, that line is lost in the undulations of the Holyoke range. At the western extremity of this range, Mt. Holyoke itself—one of the favorite mountain resorts of New England—stands out like the last gate-tower of some broken Cyclopean wall. Far in the north, like another similar tower, stands Sugar-Loaf Mountain. Between the two the whole west lies open; not indeed as a plain, but as a valley whose farther slope rises gently to the sky, broken here and there by low, intermediate hills, one of the most prominent of which is Mt. Warner. Through this valley flows the Connecticut, revealing itself here and there in silvery glimpses. In the middle distance lies Hadley, folded in by a broad curve in the river. Beyond is Northampton, so long the home of President Edwards. This whole valley is often, during the autumnal season, shrouded in morning mists, which, leveled above by the upper winds, spread out like a sea. Then Holyoke becomes a mountain shore, Mt. Warner an island. The glow-

ing maples, touched by recent frosts, and showing
themselves in some places above the surface of the
lake of cloud, appear to rest like clumps of flowers
upon its bosom. Here and there a lofty pine shows
its top, like a ship becalmed, its sails all spread.
The sun quickly dissolves the vision; but the memory of it lingers in the mind of the beholder for
many a day.

The President's house, in which all the younger
children of our family were born, was a square
brick structure, which still stands under its sycamore
shades in the heart of the village. When Dr. Humphrey assumed the presidency, the college could
boast of but a single building, which was used for
a variety of purposes. The village meeting-house,
a weather-beaten structure, stained or mottled by
dark yellow paint, stood directly opposite the College Hall, on the spot now occupied by the Cabinet
and Observatory. This structure we well remember as the Sunday resort of our boyhood. The
entrance was through the base of the steeple, in the
summit of which swung the village bell. The pews
were square, and surmounted far above the heads
of children by an open railing. Once penned for
the Sabbath service, there was no escape from the
enclosure; there was no outlook except toward the
pulpit or the ceiling. The floor was uncarpeted;

the seats were without cushions. The Benjamin of
the household generally carried to meeting in winter the mother's foot-stove, quite as sacred to him
as Prayer-Book or Bible are to some modern worshipers. In summer, he was sometimes allowed to
carry a few branches of fennel from the garden, for
his solace as the sermon went on. This venerable
meeting-house gave way before long to the church,
which, with ambitious pretentions to Grecian art,
arose not far away. This has been superseded in
its turn. The College Chapel and the Second Dor-
mitory were also erected very soon after the inauguration of the new President.

XXI.

TO give an idea of the condition of the Institution in 1823, of its original design and its early
struggles, we condense an account of its foundation
from " Historical Sketches" prepared by Dr. Humphrey in his later days, at the request of the Trustees
of the College :

" There were several years of preparatory work,
before the vision of an established college, with full
powers and franchises, gladdened the hearts of its
founders. They felt the want of an academy in
Amherst for the education of their own children, and
of others who might wish to enjoy its privileges.

Accordingly, in the month of July, 1812, a subscription was opened to erect a suitable edifice for such a school. With the avails of this and other free-will offerings the building soon went up, and in due time was opened with highly encouraging prospects, with a corps of competent teachers. In the winter of 1816, an Act of Incorporation was obtained. The aim of the corporators was high. They determined to have an academy of the very first class. To this end, November 8, 1817, a project was presented and adopted, for increasing the usefulness of the Academy, by a fund for the gratuitous education of pious young men for the ministry. It was at once resolved to establish a Professorship for instruction in the Languages; also to organize a plan for raising the proposed fund.

"The plan, however, failed, because too narrow to reach the end in view. A new one was adopted, which involved the raising of a Charity Fund of fifty thousand dollars. While subscriptions to this Fund were being taken, it was proposed by the friends of Williams College to remove that institution from Berkshire to one of the more central counties of the State. Overtures were made from Amherst, looking toward a union of the Academy with Williams College, at Amherst, or some other convenient point. Negotiations followed, but resulted in nothing. The friends of Amherst felt pressed to carry out their original idea of an Institution specially for the education of indigent young men for the ministry. This they finally resolved upon; still leaving open the door for further negotiations with Williams. Williams College was never removed; and from this beginning Amherst College grew into being. Its aim was from the first, benevolent and evangelical in a high degree. The corner-stone of its first building was laid, August 9, 1820."

The erection of this building is thus described by Dr. Humphrey:

"The committee proceeded to execute the trust committed to them, secured a title to the land, marked out the ground for the site of a building one hundred feet in length, and invited the inhabitants of Amherst, friendly to the design, to contribute labor and materials, with provisions for the workmen. With this request, the inhabitants of Amherst and a few from Pelham and Leverett most cheerfully complied. The stone for the foundations was brought chiefly from Pelham by gratuitous labor, and provisions for the workmen were furnished by voluntary contributions. The work went on so rapidly, that on the nineteenth day from the laying of the corner-stone the roof was on." The building

8

was four stories in height, and was commenced with scarcely a dollar in the treasury.

The number of students when President Humphrey was inaugurated was one hundred and twenty-six. The following schedule, taken from the cover of his inaugural address, is, in many respects, instructive and interesting:

AMHERST COLLEGIATE INSTITUTION.

FACULTY.

REV. HEMAN HUMPHREY, D. D., S. T. P., *President.*

REV. GAMALIEL S. OLDS, *Professor of Mathematics and Natural Philosophy.*

JOSEPH ESTABROOK, A. M., *Professor of Latin and Greek Languages.*

REV. JONAS KING, A. M., *Professor of Oriental Literature (to be absent for two years).*

ZENAS CLAPP, A. B., *Tutor and Librarian.*

SAMUEL M. WORCESTER, A. B., *Tutor.*

STUDENTS IN THE INSTITUTION,
OCTOBER, 1823.

SENIOR CLASS	19
JUNIOR CLASS	29
SOPHOMORE CLASS	41
FRESHMAN CLASS	37
Total	126

Hopefully pious Students, 98

From Massachusetts, 79, Connecticut, 21, New Hampshire, 10, Vermont, 4, New York, 7, New Jersey, 1, Pennsylvania, 1, South Carolina, 1, Kentucky, 1, Mississippi, 1.

That President Humphrey was introduced into no sinecure is made clear by a simple rehearsal of the duties assigned to him. He instructed the Senior Class in Rhetoric, Logic, Natural Theology, The Evidences of Christianity, Intellectual and Moral Philosophy, and Political Economy. He also presided at the weekly declamations in the chapel, and criticised the compositions of one or two of the classes. He preached on the Sabbath, occasionally, in the village meeting-house, where, until the college chapel was finished, the students worshiped. After the chapel was completed, in 1827, he supplied its pulpit regularly for two or three years, being relieved, however, in his educational duties, by the appointment of a Professor of Rhetoric. He was installed pastor of the College church on its formation, March 7, 1826. One paragraph we give from the close of his address upon this occasion :

" You will permit me to congratulate the friends of the Redeemer and of the College upon the transactions of this solemn and interesting occasion. The Institution is now at length fully organized. A church is established, which, we trust, will never be moved, on whose ample records the names of unborn thousands will be enrolled, in answer to whose prayers tens of thousands will be brought into the kingdom of Christ, and by the instrumentality of whose sons the Gospel will be carried to the ends of the earth."

The anticipations of that day have already been in great measure fulfilled.

After two or three years the pastoral labors of President Humphrey were somewhat lightened by the assistance of the Professors, all except one of whom were clergymen; and who, each in turn, alternated with him in the supply of the pulpit, and in the delivery of the regular Thursday evening lecture. He was also gradually relieved of a part of the burdens of instruction. But his labors as a President, seeking to procure a charter and a suitable endowment for the College, were multiplied. Even his vacations were almost wholly spent in this slow and vexatious work.

XXII.

WE have already seen how the earlier applications to the Legislature for a charter were defeated. A few leaves from an address delivered by Dr. Humphrey to the Alumni of the College,

August, 1853, will reveal a part of the toil and the triumph of his labors :

" The prospect of our ever succeeding was anything but encouraging. The powerful friends of both Harvard and Williams thought that a third college was not wanted; besides, there were local jealousies and competitions which seemed insuperable. The great majority of the representatives from our own county were arrayed in opposition, and used all their eloquence to prevent the incorporation. Even half the town of Amherst was opposed to the location and voted against us. Still, the petitioners determined to persevere. They put the Institute, with its four classes and regular course of college studies, under the wing of the charter of Amherst Academy. At the next winter session of the General Court, the application was renewed, and prevailed in the Senate, but was defeated by a large majority in the House. Hope deferred made the hearts of many of the students sick. We could give them no diplomas, however worthy they might be of the highest college honors. In looking back upon those dark days, I wonder they did not leave us in a body and go elsewhere. Nothing but a providential *esprit de corps* could have kept the classes unbroken.

" At that time our Legislature held two sessions in
8 *

a year. In the spring of 1824 the petitioners were
again promptly on the ground. At their request I
appeared before a joint committee of the two Houses,
and in a speech of some two hours argued the
cause as well as I was able. In the debate which followed, it was manifest that our petition was gaining
friends, and those who opposed it seemed afraid to
come to a direct vote. To stave off the question
and ultimately defeat us, they had a commission appointed, with ample powers to come to Amherst,
call the petitioners before them, look into the state
of the funds, inquire by what means they had been
obtained, and report at the next winter session. The
committee was constituted of five members of the
lower House, none of whom harmonized with us in
our religious faith ; and not one of whom, I believe,
was known to be in favor of giving us a charter. It
was confidently predicted by many, that this *search-
warrant* would settle the question against us, by
showing that the pecuniary basis on which we relied
was fictitious.

" Our next business, therefore, was, to prepare for
the investigation. We never claimed to have any
endowment, except a subscription of $50,000, as a
permanent fund, to help educate indigent pious
young men for the ministry ; and although this was
a *bona fide* subscription, a large part of which had

been paid, it was not in the best condition to abide
the searching inquisition of the legislative committee. As none of the subscribers were holden unless
the sum was made up to $50,000, several indi-
viduals were obliged, after all the papers were returned, to guarantee the deficiency, which amounted
to about $15,000. This guarantee they made in
good faith; but as they had already subscribed very
liberally, it was understood that they must be relieved as soon as other subscriptions could be obtained. Besides this, it was known that some of the
subscribers to the fund refused to pay, alleging that
they were deceived by the agents who circulated the
papers. It was deemed essential by the trustees
that the $15,000 should be lifted from the shoulders
of the warrantors before the committee came upon
the ground, and this was no easy task. The question was, where, after having turned every stone,
the trustees should look for so much money, and in
so short a time. At their request I went to Boston,
laid the case before a select meeting of our friends,
and in a few days obtained about half the sum which
was wanted. The rest was made up by the trustees,
faculty and other friends in Amherst and vicinity.
The investigating committee notified us of the time
when we might expect them. As the day drew
near, a gentleman called upon our treasurer, with

an order from the chairman of the investigating committee, to submit our subscription list to his inspection. The demand was referred by the treasurer to our prudential committee. Upon consultation they could not precisely see by what right or authority our papers were thus prematurely demanded. They accordingly directed me to return this answer:

" ' We cannot comply with this demand, for these among other important reasons : First. We do not understand how any one has a right to send for our papers, or in any way to interfere in the proposed investigation, whatever interest he may profess to represent.

" ' Secondly. By adverting to the resolution of the House of Representatives, June 10, 1824, appointing the investigating committee, we find that said committee is empowered to meet at such time and place as they may think proper, previously to the next session of the General Court, and to send for persons and papers. But we do not find that the committee is empowered by the aforesaid resolve, to call for our papers previously to their meeting, or indeed at any other time, for the purpose of putting them into the hands of any other persons.

" ' Thirdly. If the committee had been so empowered, we believe they have never acted on the subject, and, of course, that the present call for our papers does not come from them.

" ' Fourthly. The chairman of said committee has given public notice in the newspapers that they will meet in Amherst, on the fourth day of October, at which time and place all persons interested in the investigation may be heard. Of course, the Trustees of the Collegiate Institution are allowed all the time till then to arrange their papers and prepare for the investigation; and they will doubtless endeavor to have everything ready to be laid before the committee.'

" This satisfied ourselves, at least, and we heard no more of the order; the agent was left to execute his commission as best he could, without our help.

" When the day of trial came, a lawyer employed for the purpose was promptly on the ground to cross-question us in the investigation, and as a volunteer to assist the Legislative Commission in searching the matter to the bottom. All our papers were promptly put into the hands of the committee, and the investigation lasted a fortnight. Our principal agent in obtaining the subscriptions was present, and closely questioned. A lawyer who had been employed to look up testimony to condemn us, was also there, with the affidavits which he had industriously collected; and at his request, a large number of subpœnas were sent out to bring in dissatisfied subscribers.

"No similar investigation, I believe, was ever more thoroughly conducted; and some incidents in the progress of it were quite amusing to the spectators. Among the papers examined were notes to a considerable amount, which were protested by the counsel against us on the score of irresponsibility. The first was a note of a hundred dollars, and as soon as it was objected to, S. V. S. Wilder, Esq., one of our Trustees, advanced to the table and said, 'Mr. Chairman, I will cash that note,' and laid down the money. Another was produced as doubtful. 'I will cash that, too!' said he, and laid down the bills. And so of a third; and if I remember rightly, a fourth, till the chairman interposed and said, with some warmth, 'We did not come here to collect money for you.' Whereupon Mr. Wilder, bowing gracefully to the chair, put up his pocketbook.

"I have said that there were a good many small subscriptions to the fund, by minors, and other persons. These, of course, went into the hands of the committee with the rest, to make up the fifty thousand dollars. On these, it was obvious at a glance, there might be very considerable loss. This advantage against us could not escape gentlemen so astute

as our learned opponents. It was reported, and I
believe it was true, that they sat up nearly all
night, drawing off names and figuring, so as to be
ready in the morning. Getting an inkling of what
they were about, two of our Trustees drew up an
obligation, assuming the whole amount, whatever it
might be, and had it ready to. meet the expected
report. No sooner was the session opened than the
report was laid upon the table, with an air of satisfaction which seemed to say, 'Here, gentlemen
petitioners, is a poser for you.' I leave you to im-
agine what a change of countenances there was
when the guarantee was instantly produced and
read.

"The appointment of this commission proved a
real windfall to the institution. It gave the Trustees
opportunity publicly to vindicate themselves against
the aspersions which had been industriously cast
upon them, and constrained them to place the
Charity Fund on a sure foundation.

"The investigation, to be sure, cost us some time
and trouble; but it was worth more to us than a new
subscription of ten thousand dollars. I really do
not see how the sum could have been made up, in
cash, as it was on paper, without it. There were
those, and some men of renown, who 'meant not
so, neither did their heart think so.'

"Soon after the opening of the next winter session we went to Boston to hear the report of the committee. When we arrived, what was our surprise, to find that a large number of printed affidavits had been smuggled into the House and laid upon the seats of the members, setting forth various reasons for declining to pay their subscriptions. The committee, nevertheless, reported in favor of giving us a charter; and then came on the final struggle. The debate was long and earnest; and when the vote was called for, the result seemed very doubtful. But it prevailed. The charter was granted, with the names of a good Board of Trustees to carry into effect its provisions. Great rejoicings and an illumination quickly followed, and the college was duly organized by the choice of a Faculty.

"The charter was a God-send to the institution. It brought us into the honorable sisterhood of New England colleges, and though the youngest of the family, not the least. The number of undergraduates rapidly increased, till in less than ten years, it rose to more than two hundred and fifty; and for several successive years stood next in number to Yale College.

"But fair and promising as the young sister was, she could get nothing to begin with from the parent who had bestowed ' never so much dowry' upon the elder.

"Though the charter gave the institution a legal existence, it was nothing more than a roll of parchment. It brought us no money, and everything was yet to be done. We had no chapel, no recitation and lecture-rooms, no library, and nothing deserving the name of an apparatus in any department. In these respects it was truly a day of small things."

The labor of procuring funds was greater than that of obtaining a charter. It was especially an irksome work, and one for which Dr. Humphrey thought himself poorly fitted.

One of the family traditions, however, shows that he had some of the requisites of a solicitor. On one of his journeys to Boston in the stage-coach of the day, the vehicle stopped at a village to take up a lady. The rain was falling—the coach was filled. The driver, opening the door, asked if any passenger would resign his seat for one on "the deck," in favor of the lady. No one moved for a moment. The next instant Dr. Humphrey was on the ground, and the lady in his place. Some time afterward, when this village was canvassed for subscriptions to the College, the husband of the lady was called upon. He looked at the subscription-list, subscribed

9   G

a handsome sum, and returned it, saying, " I do not know much about Amherst College, but I know its President is a gentleman."

The incessant toil which marked these years told severely upon even his robust constitution. His health was nearly broken, when, in the winter of 1834, some friends of the College proposed to defray the expenses of a few months' travel in Europe, for the restoration of his flagging energies. This journey was undertaken in the following spring, and was of inestimable service. A series of letters, written during that journey, and printed in the *New York Observer*, obtained a wide circulation. The paths of European travel had not then been beaten hard by American tourists.

After his return, his official duties were less burdensome than they had been. The College was favored with a full corps of eminent professors. He was, however, continually employed in some useful College labor. He was a most systematic student, and devoted many of his leisure moments to literary composition. He was a regular contributor to the religious journals of the day. He identified himself with all popular movements for true reform. His advocacy of temperance was constant and effectual. His public addresses in the pulpit and on the platform were frequent. His voice became familiar at all the great centres of benevolent effort. He was an earnest friend of the Colonization movement, so long as that promised most for the relief of the slave. The soundness of his judgment became as widely known as the mingled wisdom and eloquence of his lips. He was consulted in ecclesiastical matters far and near.

By the students in the College he was singularly revered. There are many now living, by whom President Humphrey is recollected as the embodiment of all that is wise and good. He obtained a powerful influence over the students by his personal interest in them; by his familiar lectures in the class-room to Freshmen on college-life—to schoolteachers on life in the school-room; and by his frequent fatherly counsels to all. His patience was occasionally tried by college pranks, but his wisdom and his good-humor never failed to serve him. The twinkle, or rather *gleam*, in his eye often showed that he appreciated the fun he was bound to rebuke.

One incident of the early days of the College is so characteristic and so well known that we give it in Dr. Humphrey's words :

" Two rooms in the old College had been thrown together for a temporary chapel, with a small, rough desk at one end, in which, I suppose, it was thought a good joke early to try one's metal, and see whether

it would ring or not. Accordingly one morning, as
I came in to prayers, I found the chair preoccupied
by a goose. She looked rather shabby to be sure,
but nevertheless was a veritable goose. Strange as
it may seem, she did not salute me with so much as
a hiss for my unceremonious intrusion. It might be
because I did not offer to *take the chair*. As anybody might venture to stand a few moments, even in
such a presence, I carefully drew the chair up behind me as closely as I safely could, went through
the exercises, and the students retired in the usual
orderly manner ; not more than two or three, I believe, having noticed anything uncommon. In the
course of the day it was reported that as soon as
they found out what had happened they were highly
excited, and proposed calling a college meeting to
express their indignation that such an insult had
been offered by one of their number. The hour of
evening prayers came, and at the close of the usual
exercises, I asked the young gentlemen to be seated
a moment ; stated what I had heard, and thanked
them for the kind interest they had taken in the
matter ; told them it was just what I should expect
from gentlemen of such high, honorable feelings ;
but begged them not to give themselves the least
trouble in the premises. ' You know,' I said, ' that
the Trustees have just been here to organize a Col-

lege Faculty. Their intention was to provide competent instructors in all the departments, so as to
meet the capacity of every student. They thought
they had done so. But it seems that *one* student
was overlooked, and I am sure they will be glad to
learn that he has promptly supplied the deficiency
by choosing a goose for his tutor. *Par nobile
fratrum.'"*

XXIV.

THE foregoing pages afford but a faint conception
of the early labors devolved upon the President
of Amherst College. The anxieties which attended
the obtaining of a charter can never be appreciated
by those who simply read the history of the institution. No pen could ever record the long confer-
ences, the perplexed thoughts, the fearful appre-
hensions, the wearying vexations which excited the
brain and wore on the nerves of one whose whole
heart was given to this enterprise. Nor can any
mere reader understand how much was involved in
the earlier efforts made by President Humphrey to
procure funds for the College when it had received
its charter. Week after week was taken from the
time appropriated to collegiate duty for this purpose. Vacation after vacation was consumed in this
work, which was, in some respects, more wearying

9 *

than that of appeal to a Legislature. To plead for rights is one thing; to ask for charities is another. It is true, that such charities as these are, in one sense, rights. All men are God's stewards, and a just plea for benevolence is a plea for the rights of the Master. But he who stands firmest in this conviction is unable to forget, as he urges his claim, that all solicitors for benevolent objects are regarded as in some degree like all askers of alms. Comparatively few of those who give for benevolence give as if the act were a privilege. The freest givers are so continually plied with arguments from every side that it is necessary to convince them by cogent reasonings that they may, conscientiously, devote to one object what is claimed for another. Besides, it is well understood that the earlier endowments of a collegiate institution are, almost always, obtained with far more difficulty than the later ones. Here, as elsewhere, the law prevails, "Whosoever hath to him shall be given;" and there is continual fear that "Whosoever hath not, from him shall be taken even that which he seemeth to have." "How do I know that my hundreds, given to an enterprise which is yet so feeble as to be of doubtful life, may not be cast into the sea?" is a natural question. "My thousands given to an enterprise which has already the elements of an enduring life, will be like new stones in a temple which will stand for centuries," is a natural argument.

Had President Humphrey no further honor than this, that he secured the launching and the dress of his ship, and piloted it out of a crooked harbor into the open sea, that were enough for one who beholds Amherst College as it now is. But his honor is greater than this. He, more than any one else, was instrumental in giving the College its character. Under his administration the purpose of its founders was realized. They desired it to be a training-school for the Church, a seminary for the education especially of ministers and missionaries of the Cross. That this desire might be realized was the cogent motive which drew him from the pastorate in Pittsfield. A single paragraph, already quoted from his address at the foundation of the College church, shows how earnest was his sympathy in this desire. We give another paragraph, taken from the close of his inaugural address, as pervaded by the same feeling:

"As we cast our eyes down the long track of time, from this consecrated eminence, how many bright and interesting visions crowd upon our view! We, indeed, shall soon be gone; but other generations will come, and what may they not enjoy and accomplish, canopied as they will be by these Arcadian

skies, invigorated by the pure breath of the mountains, and inspired to rapture and to song as they
look abroad upon all the riches, life and beauty of
this great amphitheatre? How many favored sons
of this institution will hold sweet converse here with
the muse that loves the hill of Zion! How many
statesmen, historians and orators will be trained on
this ground to shine in senates, to grace the bar, to
adorn the bench of justice, and to record the doings
of the wise, the brave and the good! But more
than all that has been mentioned, what may not this
seminary do for the churches at home; what victo-
ries may she not gain in distant lands, by sending
forth her sons under the banner of the Cross, and
clad in armor of heavenly temper to fight the battles
of her King?

"Who is there in this assembly that is not ready
to answer, May these glowing anticipations be more
than realized in the future prosperity and usefulness
of this institution? May it live to gladden and
bless the Church through all future generations, and
in that world where holiness is perfect and knowledge is transcendent, may all its founders, patrons
and friends meet and dwell together for ever in the
presence of God and the Lamb."

Let any one who is curious to see what order of
students has come from this institution, study its

last Triennial, see what distinguished names are on
its roll, and how many of those names are printed
in the honored *italics* which designate ministers of
the Gospel.

President Humphrey was successful in impressing
all students by the force of his own character. One
of the most widely-known preachers in America has
more than once borne public testimony that, while
in Amherst College, he was more influenced by the
President as a man than even as an instructor. His
personal character was like an atmosphere or a sun-
shine. What he was, the College, to a great extent, became.

That he was continually solicitous for the religious
interests of the institution, is evidenced by his activity in promoting the frequent revivals which occurred
under his administration. In his address to the
Alumni in 1853, he said:

"There is nothing which I look back upon during
my connection with the College, with so much satisfaction and so many thanksgivings to God, as 'the
times of refreshing from his presence' which we enjoyed. I have ever regarded them as so many
testimonies of the Divine approbation of the motives
of its founders. They meant to make it a College
for Christ and the Church; and that it might remain
so, was, I have no doubt, the burden of their pray-

ers. By this hope they were cheered in the darkest
times, and in every revival they greatly rejoiced.
Of how many will it be said, when Christ makes
up his jewels, This and that pastor or missionary
was born there! It seems to me the richest smile
of Heaven upon Amherst College, that no class has
ever graduated without having passed at least once
under the cloud which has so often 'poured out
righteousness' upon it. If, in its former straits,
every drop had been fine gold, how meagre the
blessing compared with the effusions of the Holy
Spirit by which the Church has been refreshed, and
in which so many sinners have been converted to
God! I shall never forget the charge I received
when I was installed pastor of the church. 'Contend earnestly for the Faith once delivered to the
saints,' said the venerable father upon whom that
duty devolved. 'We would rather come here to
bury you than that you should depart from the true
faith.' So I now say: Let this College be swept
from under these glorious heavens sooner than any
other Gospel shall be preached within these walls
than that which has been made 'the wisdom of God
and the power of God' to the salvation of so many
souls!"

It had long been his declared intention to retire
from some of his more responsible trusts when his

threescore years should be rounded. "At sixty,"
he would say, "a man may still be vigorous; in
some respects he may be more efficient than ever;
but he cannot be so sure of his mental operations
as in middle life." He was already sixty-five when
he felt constrained to resign the office he had held
for twenty-two years. The College had long been
a recognized power in the land. He felt that it
could be safely committed to a new leadership.

In April, 1845, he tendered his resignation, and
made his arrangements to retire from collegiate life.
He has been followed by able and distinguished
men; the first of his successors, Pres. Edward
Hitchcock, being then already known as among the
foremost *savants* of the scientific world.

He did not, however, retire into an idle repose.
His residence was fixed for the most of the ensuing
year with Rev. Henry Neill, at Hatfield, Massachusetts, but his time was largely occupied by revival labors and by the supply of vacant congregations in the neighborhood.

XXV.

Where now should be the home of his old age?
His former parishioners in Pittsfield plead for his
return to them—not now as pastor, but as friend.

He yields, and to this place of fond memories returns for the evening of life. A new house near his former residence was procured, and he was soon at home again among those who welcomed him with all their old affection. For a few years the numerous demands made upon him by the churches drew him frequently from his family. He supplied vacant pulpits, assisted his brethren in extraordinary labors, traveled through Western Massachusetts to rouse new interest in the cause of Missions, and delivered several lectures in behalf of the American Colonization Society, principally in New York and Boston. His face was as familiar as ever on anniversary platforms. And while at home his pen was more nimble than ever. He visited his children at Louisville, and at Milwaukee, as well as at Lenox, Binghamton and New York. He made summer tours for health and pleasure. He revisited his old haunts and homes in Connecticut. Scarcely any young man was more active than he. Gradually, however, he fell into a more reposeful life, still retaining his interest in all the movements of society, and resuming the regular habits which had characterized his yonnger days. In the early summer morning we used to hear the click of his hoe in the garden. In the evening we were his companions as he took his regular walk. In winter mornings he substituted the study of the Scriptures for the early physical exercise. After breakfast and family devotion the study was his resort. There, from nine o'clock until the bell struck for dinner, he spent the hours in writing; sometimes a chapter of a book, sometimes a communication from "The Old Man of the Mountains," sometimes a letter to a friend, or a few pages of a sermon or of autobiographical reminiscence. The results of these continued literary labors can only be appreciated by those who review the accumulations of his unremitted toil. After dinner came miscellaneous reading, of new books, of current periodicals and newspapers, "to keep up with the times." Then came the walk, the visit, the genial talk with friend or family. After tea the religious meeting, or the friendly call, given or received. Then as ten o'clock approached, the familiar Bible was produced, the fervent prayer was offered, and soon after was heard the whirr of the wheels in the tall old clock in the hall, as he wound it for another twenty-four hours of faithful service.

By such regular habits the health of both body and mind was wonderfully preserved. He was seldom even partially disabled by illness. His sleep was almost never disturbed. Uniformly cheerful, and seeming to our partial eyes more

10

and more genial as the mellow sunset came on, he contributed greatly to the happiness of all about him.

All village affairs interested him. When he returned to Pittsfield from Amherst, he found that the old church whose severed parts had been so kindly knit again under his ministry, had become so large that division was now as much a duty as union had been twenty-eight years before. A colony was soon formed. He identified himself with this colony in a spirit of rare self-sacrifice, as most of his former friends remained in the First Church. A new house of worship was provided for the colony, largely in consequence of his influence and exertions. A pastor was installed—one of the choicest in New England—Rev. Dr. Harris, now President of Bowdoin College, Maine. Dr. Humphrey returned to the First Church a few years afterward, when his mission in the colony appeared to be accomplished.

He interested himself greatly in the establishment of a Public Library, which is now large, and of great benefit to the village. He promoted also a "Tree-Planting Association." A coming generation will rejoice in shade which he was instrumental in providing. Thus his influence was felt in many a healthful touch given to all the springs of village life and prosperity. To the last, he was the friend and the counselor of the young. He prepared a series of sermons to this class of society, which he loved to deliver wherever he had opportunity. They were listened to by hundreds with eager attention. In 1859, as he rounded his eightieth year, he prepared a sermon on "Old Age," which he delivered in the First Church at the request of the pastor, Rev. J. Todd, D.D., who always revered him, and who was loved in return. This sermon, full of pleasant reminiscences, is marked by nothing so much as by the interest it reveals in those who are fresh in the circuit of life.

The citizens of Pittsfield maintained the warmth of the welcome with which they had greeted him on his return, to the very end. Those who had not known him as pastor soon learned to respect him as citizen and love him as friend. The children of his former parishioners seemed to have brought such memories of him out of their forming years, that they regarded him with a reverence as nearly saintly as is consistent with Puritan character. The tributes of respect and affection he continually received were very precious to him, and will always be remembered as precious by his children. He used to say, as he walked about the village, "All these lawns and gardens are mine;" referring only to the pleasure he derived from them, and the freedom with

which all these gates were open to his foot: "The
are mine without the trouble and expense of takin
care of them." Very often, in his walks, he woul
enter the highly-cultivated grounds of some neigh
bor, and wander for a time among the glowing bed
or under the drooping boughs, feeling that sense o
ownership which was derived from the thought tha
God paints his tints and distills his odors for all hi
children; and from the consciousness that were h
known to wish it, no flower or fruit would be s
precious as to be refused him. Indeed, his parlo
and his table bore continual witness that "all gar
dens were his." It was no formal tribute—it wa
but the natural sequel of all that had gone before
that when at last his dust was borne to the grave
the stores along the line of the procession wer
closed, all the bells of the village were tolled, an
those who had abandoned all other duty, went i
solemn order to the place where the revered form
was laid. Dr. Todd spoke for many when he sai
in his funeral sermon, "It will be a rich legacy t
our children, that they can walk through our beauti
ful cemetery and point the finger and say, 'Ther
sleeps Dr. Humphrey.'"

XXVI.

ONE of the brightest points in Dr. Humphrey's domestic history during the tranquil evening of his life, was the celebration of the fiftieth anniversary of his marriage, April 20, 1858. At this "Golden Wedding" all his surviving children, nearly all of his sons and daughters-in-law, and most of his grandchildren, together with several of our more distant relatives, were present. From widely-scattered homes they came, with glad hearts and with many a significant tribute of affection. The citizens of Pittsfield expressed almost as much interest in the occasion as if they had been members of the family. Their substantial gifts are treasured among the most valued heirlooms of the house.

On the morning of the anniversary, the family were gathered in the familiar parlors to receive the greetings of the day. The family altar was surrounded by a group whose devotions were quickened by a thousand happy memories, and led in such outpourings of the soul as seldom fell from even the venerable lips of him whom all the worshipers so much revered and loved.

An address which Dr. Humphrey had previously prepared, was then read. It was full of reminiscence, and radiant in all its passages with gratitude

10 *   H

and affection. It was too personal for insertion in these pages. The written prayer with which it opened may, however, be inserted, as revealing the heart out of which it came :

" Almighty and ever blessed God, we adore thee as our Creator and Preserver. We are fearfully and wonderfully made. Thou hast endowed us with social natures as well as immortal spirits. Thou settest the solitary in families, and in thee are all the pious families of the earth blessed.

" O Lord, we thank thee for what our eyes see and our hearts feel to-day. We thank thee for this great and joyful family gathering. What hast thou wrought for us ! We are like them that dream. In great mercy hast thou spared the lives of thine unworthy servants, the united head, to number fifty years of our pilgrimage since the holy rite that made us one. We thank thee for the children whom thou hast given us. We miss some of them. They are not all here. But we thank thee that the most of them still live, and that thou hast brought them home to us with their children, on an occasion so uncommon in this dying world. And now, Lord, what wait we for but thy presence and blessing? Thy favor is life and thy loving-kindness is better than life. May this sacred hour, with its kindred reminiscences, be one of the most refreshing and profitable of our lives. May we enjoy the presence and approbation of the same Divine Guest whose smiles gladdened every heart at the marriage-feast in Cana of Galilee. May the words of our mouths and the meditations of our hearts be acceptable in thy sight, O Lord, our strength and our Redeemer. We thank thee that our hearts flow together in this great family gathering, and that there is no absent prodigal to mourn over in the midst of these joyous greetings of parents and children and children's children. May our souls be more closely knit together in bonds which can never be broken, however widely asunder our earthly lot may be cast. May we gain new strength to meet the duties and trials of life. May our whole intercourse while we are together, be such as shall secure thine approbation which is life, and thy loving-kindness which is better than life. We all feel that it is good for us to be here. It is a sweet fellowship of kindred souls, and, O Lord, we thank thee that we are allowed to rest for a few days at this stage of our earthly pilgrimage; to look back upon the ground, rugged and smooth, already passed; and leaning upon thine Almighty arm, to renew our strength for what yet lies between us and the end of the journey. Pardon all our sins and shortcomings, we humbly beseech thee. Receive us graciously and love us freely, for the sake only of our adorable Redeemer, to whom be glory for ever. Amen !"

In the evening came a throng of friends from the village to offer their congratulations. If such occasions can be dignified by a title borrowed from precious substance, it was a " golden wedding," indeed.

When the delightful days of this family reunion were spent, the children and the children's children were once more brought together for benediction and farewell. The trembling hand held the manuscript. The trembling voice pronounced the words of parting :

" Our prayers have been answered. Our lives have been spared, and God has brought you home from your wide dispersions, to gladden our aged hearts with your filial greetings, and to rejoice with us and with one another on an anniversary such as but few families are permitted to enjoy. Our cup of blessings has been more than full ; it has run over. It would be delightful to have you all build your tabernacles around us and remain. But it may not be. As Peter, James and John must come down from the Mount, and betake themselves to the rough and self-denying duties of life, under the direction of their Master, so you have homes and duties to which you must return. . . . .

"*Farewell*, notwithstanding its good meaning, is a word that lingers, reluctant to leave our lips. But this is not even your earthly rest. You must go your several ways; and may the angel of the covenant go with you! . . . . What changes may await you on the journey of life it is not granted us to foresee; and you know, 'It is not in man that walketh to direct his steps.' Trust in the Lord at all times, and lean not to your own understandings. In all your ways acknowledge him, and he shall direct your paths. . . . . As we give you, one after the other, the parting hand, we bless you in the name of the Lord. May you be shielded from all the dangers of the way, and resume your duties with renewed health and encouragements! Take care to adorn your Christian profession. We have no greater joy than that our children are walking in the truth. Serve God and your generation faithfully, according to his will; and whether we meet any more in this world or not, may we all be received as welcome guests at the Marriage Supper of the Lamb!

"And now, O Lord our Heavenly Father, go with these beloved sons and daughters, and the children thou has given them. Hitherto thou hast appointed the bounds of their habitation in great mercy. Whatever future changes of abode may await them, choose out all such changes for them; guide them by thy counsel, and screen them by thy grace. May these thy servants, the beloved heads of so many families, bring up their children in the nurture and admonition of the Lord! Fulfil to the widow and the fatherless all thy great and precious promises. Wilt thou cause the widow's heart to sing for joy; and may all their children rise up and call them blessed!

" "As they now leave us we give them a parting blessing. 'Guide them, O thou great Jehovah.' Such another meeting we shall never enjoy here below. We thank thee, and call upon our souls and all that is within us to bless thee that thou hast granted us this, so rare a favor. May we be reunited at last, an unbroken family, where they go no more out for ever. This is opening our mouths wide. It is asking for blessings infinitely great; but it is asking them in thy name, O thou infinitely great and adorable Saviour, to whom with thee, O Father, and the Holy Ghost, we will render equal and undivided praises. Amen."

So we separated, with a double benediction upon our heads, that which he pronounced and that which came in answer to his prayer.

Most of us were permitted to come, once and again, to receive the patriarchal welcome and bless-

ing before the silver cord was loosed and the golden
bowl broken.

• XXVII.

A S our father's eighty-first birth-day was ushered
in, he sat down to record some new reminiscences—some fresh expressions of gratitude, some
further outpouring of prayer. He is still strong,
but he reviews the year just closed with a careful
self-scrutiny. " I can see that my outer man has
decayed faster than in any preceding year, but I
suffer very little." " When I sit down to write, it
takes me longer to collect my thoughts than it once
did. The wings of my imagination are clipped.
But, if I am not entirely deceived, my judgment has
suffered less. I seem to be a better critic of popular
books and speakers than I was twenty years ago."
"As yet I am a stranger to depression of spirits.
I still look on the bright side of things and enjoy
cheerful society. It affords me great satisfaction, as
I am passing off the stage, to carry with me the
strong persuasion that the world is growing better."

Then follows the review of the year. Then the
prayer of which these are portions :

" I thank thee that thou hast given me this pleasant home in the bosom of my family, and surrounded
by friends whose hearts are always warm and whose

hands are often filled with testimonies of their kindly
Christian regard. I thank thee that the doors have
not been shut in the streets; that I have been able to
go out and come in; that I have not been left to
want any good thing; that I have had health regularly to go up to the House of the Lord. I thank
thee, O divine Redeemer, that I have so often during
the year enjoyed the privilege of showing forth thy
death at thy table. I mourn that I have not loved
thee more and served thee better. I lament the
poor returns I have made to thee for thy boundless
love and compassion in bearing my sins upon the
cross, and in opening the fountain of thine own
precious blood to wash them all away. Oh what
infinite compassion! Oh what unspeakable mercy!
Oh what sweet and melting invitations! Oh what a
privilege to have lived another year of borrowed
time so near the gate of heaven! Oh for a thousand
tongues to praise thee for what thou art and for what
thou hast done to save a lost world!

"This day I enter upon a new year of my long
life. It may be the last. I may scarcely pass the
threshold ere the final summons comes. If so, Lord
Jesus, receive my spirit! If I am spared a little
longer, teach me so to number my days, so to improve the time which remains, that when the mes-
senger comes I may be found with my loins girded

about and my lamp trimmed and burning. Grace; rich grace; free grace; this is all my hope, flowing, as it were, from the pierced and bleeding heart of the Lamb of God, whose blood alone cleanseth from all sin!"

The year thus opened passed as peacefully as the preceding, until, in its closing months, the storm of the Southern Rebellion rose on the sky. Dr. Humphrey's loyal heart was intensely moved by the events which so quickened the pulses of the country. His interest in public affairs was almost painful. When the clergymen of Pittsfield met to make arrangements for the day of National Fasting and Prayer, to be observed January 4, 1861, he was appointed to deliver, at a union meeting, the sermon of the day. He accepted the invitation with all the ardor of his youth. He repaired to his study on the very day of his appointment and commenced his work. His hands trembled with eagerness; his face glowed with excitement. His family remonstrated against his attempting the duty assigned to him; but he thought himself strong enough to undertake it. Could he refuse to take the pen when so many were buckling on the sword? The result was a sermon which, for argument, for eloquence, for religious and patriotic fire, was considered equal to the best efforts of his meridian days.

11

" It now lies before us," says an article in the *Independent*, " in a pamphlet published by request of Governor Briggs and other leading citizens of Pittsfield, who heard it preached ; and it seems to us in every way a remarkable discourse to have been prepared and delivered by a man standing on the edge of his eighty-third year."

It is probable that the excitement attending the preparation and delivery of this sermon depressed his vital energies, and hastened the assault of disease by which the citadel of life was beseiged and carried.

In February, while on a visit to Amherst, he experienced the first premonition of danger. He treated it lightly, as but the consequence of the intense cold of the season. It was but a difficulty in breathing which disturbed his sleep. Soon after his return to Pittsfield he suffered from a recurrence of the unpleasant symptom. This time no reason could be found in the temperature. The difficulty returned again and again. It became alarming. Yet it is significant of his energy of character, that he maintained the customary round of his life ; and while so much distressed by panting lungs and shattered nerves that he could not guide his pen, he dictated to one of his family a communication for a newspaper conducted by one of his grandchildren,

Ere long, he was prostrated by an attack so severe that for the time his life was despaired of.

XXVIII.

EARLY in March, his absent children were startled by telegraphic summons to Pittsfield. They hastened thither, scarcely expecting to find him living. The assault, however, had been successfully resisted. His constitution, so strongly braced and invigorated by early care and lifelong prudence, was not easily overpowered. For several days after the collection of the family he was able to be with them, occasionally, at the table or at the family altar. But the conflict with death had evidently begun. He lingered for nearly a month, gradually becoming weaker. It was like the pounding of a well-riveted ship upon the beach on which it is cast, losing mast and sail and the lighter fabrics of the deck, rocking in the breakers, striking in the stormier days with a force which threatened an immediate parting of bolt and rib and knee, yet resisting all with a wonderful power.

At first his mind was clear. He understood his danger, but for several days after his physicians regarded his case as almost hopeless no such announcement was made to him. He was still able to move from room to room, when, by one of his sons who has now rejoined him in glory, he was told that the end was near. For a moment he was startled. An expression of the most intense solemnity then overspread his countenance as, for the moment, he gave himself up to the thought of standing before a holy God. Soon afterward he retired to his room and gathered about him his family for the prayer and counsel of dying breath.

The first characteristics of his religious experience in view of death were such as one might naturally expect, when considering the type of his conversion, his early theological training, his remarkable conscientiousness, and his equally remarkable humility. The thought of God's perfect holiness was one of the grandest in his creed. He, before whom the heavens are unclean, and who chargeth his angels with folly—he who cannot look upon sin but with abhorrence, was now to be the Judge of one who was acutely sensitive to his own shortcomings—who often in his prayer felt like laying his hand upon his mouth and his mouth in the dust, while far above him he heard the chant of the angels, "Holy, holy, holy Lord God Almighty!"

"How can I, how can any mortal, stand before God?"

The thought of Christ as a perfect sacrifice then

came to his relief, and he expressed his confidence in the redemption he has provided. He did not tremble in anticipation of the judgment, but felt humbled that his character would stand out in such contrast to that of his Judge. After a time this feeling gave way to those softer and more glowing experiences which centre themselves upon Christ the glorified Saviour, rather than upon the holy Judge. Thenceforth the humility of the conscious sinner blended with the glad anticipations of the saint, redeemed by the precious blood of the Lamb.

Gradually his mind became clouded. The disease, which made his breathing often paroxysmal, deprived the blood of oxygen, and so disturbed the brain. Sometimes in a lucid interval he would give some parting instruction or say some parting word. He would send a farewell to an absent one, or turning to the wife—anxiously seeking to soothe and help him—would say, " I trust we shall spend long ages together in heaven. To dwell with Christ—that will be heaven !" Then some expression like this would drop from his lips : " To love and serve God for ever, without any imperfection—how different from the imperfect service I have rendered here !"

" It doth not yet appear what we shall be ; but we shall see him as he is, and be for ever with

11 *

the Lord for ever and ever and ever with the Lord; worship him—glory inexpressible—nothing but glory and happiness in the face of Jesus Christ!"

"A glimpse of that glory, how wonderful! Everlasting happiness, and this just upon the dying-bed of the believer!—I stand and contemplate this blessedness, and am filled with rapture and love—O glory! O heaven! O bliss!—Abounding grace and mercy in Jesus Christ!"

Sometimes, when water was given him, and which he continually craved, he would smile and refer to a spring which flowed near his father's house in Barkhamstead. Like David of old, he thought of the spring where he slaked the thirst of his boyhood, as the sweetest in the world. Oh for a draught from that hill-side fountain! "But then," he would add, "how much sweeter will be the river of the water of life which flows from beneath the Throne of God and of the Lamb!"

At times we could hardly decide whether his expressions were those of a collected or of a wandering mind; but always they showed his strong character, his unyielding faith, and his trust in the redeeming blood of Christ.

"My own powers of investigation are entirely broken down. I have nothing to do with metaphysical investigations—nothing to come between me and the cross of Christ."

"In days past, truly what comforts and deliverances have there been !"

"God, help me to soar—to soar—to soar away to glory, honor and immortality for ever !"

"Draw out my faith and love in far more rapturous strains !"

"Why should I linger any longer here, O Divine and adorable Redeemer! What should keep me back?"

In one of his more clouded moments he imagined that his spirit had already escaped the clay. Then the obscure consciousness of his suffering gave a tone of disappointment to his expressions.

"I confess that I had expected more of the glories, and of the immediate opening of the heavenly world, and less of the trial after death."

But soon the disappointment gave way to experiences such as these expressions reveal : "Blessed be God for his eternal rest !—It is so unexpected to see these glories and hear that music !—Swallowed up and lost !"

"Glorious things !" cried he, on another occasion. "Who could desire more? And where is the crown? Where is the seat of the Saviour's kingdom?"

It is impossible to describe those heavy-footed days in which he lingered in waiting for his release. But they ended at last on Wednesday, April 3. He passed his eighty-second birth-day in suffering, just a week before. We had almost hoped that would be the day of his departure, that thus the earthly might run evenly into the heavenly calendar. Perhaps that last week of the "tribulation" out of which he "came" at length, was important to the perfecting of his glory among those who have "made white their robes in the blood of the Lamb."

Another pen has told the rest of the story. In the funeral sermon by Rev. Dr. Todd—a discourse so eloquent in thought and feeling, so just and discriminating in its tributes to Dr. Humphrey's memory—is this passage:

"His last sickness was an exhibition of one of the mysteries of our nature, when disease preys upon the nerves with a power which no medical skill can control, and which seems to make the whole body a collection of diseased cords—not one of which can be quieted till the body and intellect are overpowered—a state most painful to bear, and hardly less so to witness. For the most part the reason was clouded; but even then, in the dark prison-house, his spirit was feeling after the pillars

of truth and searching for her accustomed light.
Samson, in the prison-house, dark and dreary, is
noble, even there. At one time, in the mazes of a
beclouded intellect—tempted, as he thought, to
apostatize—he told his imaginary tempter: ' No, I
cannot become a Jew !' And as the trial was crowd-
ing harder, and he felt that he was persecuted to
turn Mohammedan, he said, with his own emphatic
voice and manner, ' No amount of suffering, mental
or physical, will make me turn Mohammedan !' and
then added—and in the circumstances of the case it
was sublime—' I know in whom I have believed ! I
know that my Redeemer liveth ! I stand upon the
Rock of Ages !'

"At another time, when a friend intimated to him
that his end was near, he seemed to start up out
of the lethargy, the cloud at once lifted, reason
rallied to her throne, and for a few minutes, like the
dying Jacob, he sat up, called for his wife and children to come around him, when he gave to each a
few words of love—more precious than jewels—and
sent special messages to absent children and friends.
It was the sun breaking out between the evening
clouds—clear, soft and beautiful. In a few moments
he fell back, and the bright daylight was gone ; and
when the spirit again became conscious, she was in
unclouded, everlasting day. When the hour of

I

dismissal came, the angel of death walked the room so softly that his steps were not heard. Like David of old, 'he fell on sleep,' as on a pillow, and the only difference to him between sleep and death was, that in the one case the bosom barely heaved, and in the other it was still, and the prophecy was fulfilled, 'Thou shalt come to thy grave in a full age, like as a shock of corn cometh in in his season!' and the great prayer of the Redeemer was answered —'Father, I will that those whom thou hast given me, be with me where I am, that they may behold my glory.'"

The funeral was attended, April 8, from the Congregational Church. The building was heavily draped in black. An immense concourse was present. The services were conducted by several clergymen. And when the benediction was pronounced, the last look at the peaceful face was taken. Then the long procession, then the words of burial, then the rounded grave. Now the granite monument, inscribed with a favorite text of him whose dust reposes beneath it:

INCREASING IN THE KNOWLEDGE OF GOD.

Now, also, ten thousand precious memories; countless influences; words that cannot die; a character which stands, strong and shapely, where thought sets up its models, one of the few realities among our ideals of human excellence and symmetry.

Having thus imperfectly traced the connected line of Dr. Humphrey's history, it still remains to delineate analytically his characteristics. In attempting this we are fully aware of the difficulty besetting the partial pen of a son. Yet there is an advantage in the intimacy of a child which no stranger could ever enjoy. Public men are often studied from the distance, somewhat as the astronomer of to-day studies the planets. We have maps and globes representing Mars. We are told of the snows at its poles, and of the seas and continents which clothe its milder zones. An inhabitant of the planet—if such there be—could tell us far more of his world than an earthly astronomer could ever learn, though his glasses were never so powerful. In the use of that knowledge which is derived from the most intimate relations to our subject, we shall endeavor to be impartial; we shall be pardoned if we overdraw.

THE MAN.

In physical constitution he was unusually strong and vigorous. He was subject to few maladies, was haunted by no chronic disorder, and was seldom prostrated by acute disease. The vital machinery ran on for eighty years, with scarcely an interruption in its regular movements. He was of bilious temperament, and so well balanced, that while seldom unduly excited, he was as seldom unduly depressed. He was never so much burdened by care that he could not sleep through the hours of repose. His load was never carried beyond the door of his bed-chamber. In person, he was of medium height and well developed. His eye was dark and mild. His hair, in earlier life, was black, and curled about the high and rounded " dome of thought," which, in later years, was smooth, from eyebrow to summit. Till past middle life his face was full and ruddy. He was fond of physical exertion, and never abandoned it. The habits of the farmer clung to him to the last. Throughout the period of his presidency he conducted a small farm, the operations of which he always found time to oversee.

It is related of Rev. 'Dr. Emmons, that he adopted a life so sedentary that he wore holes in the floor of his study by the incessant chafing of his chair ; and that he would not abandon the " Lord's work" at the writing-table to help secure his hay, imperiled by a coming shower. We have often followed the President from the study to the hay-field, under both bright and clouded skies. No one was a better judge than he of the quality of an axe or a scythe. No one better knew where to insert a wedge into a refractory knot. He was fond of driving or rambling amid the beautiful scenery which always surrounded him. He was skillful in the use of rod and gun, though he seldom allowed himself to gratify the tastes of the sportsman. The garden, the field, the orchard, afforded him the most of his exercise.

In mental constitution he was unusually symmetrical. If any qualities were prominent, they were those which made him a man of practical wisdom and judgment. John Locke would have referred to him as an example of "roundabout sense." Dr. Todd says of him:

"A rare thing it is to find a man who has lived more than fourscore years—always in action—who has said and done so few unwise things as President Humphrey. It is an original gift. Those who have gone to him for counsel, those who have acted with him on committees or on ecclesiastical councils, those who have wrestled with him in deep discussions in ministerial meetings, those who have sat under him as an instructor or pastor, have all, without dissent, accorded to him the appellation of 'a wise man.' On all moral questions his instincts were quick and unerring. Though he made no pretensions to far-reaching views, yet all knew that

12

to follow his advice was to walk in safety. I never knew an instance where it was disregarded when the mistake was not most manifest sooner or later. You might pour over him a load of theories and opinions, and he would instantly pick out the true from the shams."

Associated with this wisdom, was an unusual tact in reading character, in discerning motives and in harmonizing conflicting feelings. His success in eradicating the Half-way Covenant from the church in Fairfield, in cementing the broken fibres of the church in Pittsfield, and in promoting the interests of Amherst College in its days of struggle, are ready illustrations.

His logical faculties were not uncommon. His reasonings were conducted more by analogy than by demonstration. Yet his deductions from facts were clear and convincing. The Baconian method was his especial favorite. Facts were the "stubborn things" out of which he loved to frame his arguments. He was not marked as an original thinker, but he was distinguished for the solid fire of talent, if not for the brilliant corruscations of genius.

He had a lively fancy, but not a powerful imagination. His writings were often as highly illuminated as a missal; but the tints of the illumination

were, like those of a missal, borrowed, though skillfully combined. So, while he had little wit, he had
an abundance of humor. This played on the surface of all his familiar conversations. It made his
after-dinner speeches on Commencement occasions
always agreeable. One of the laws of the College
was, that no firearms should be kept in the students'
rooms or used by them during term-time. We well
remember meeting him one day as he was coming
down the College hill, with a gun on each shoulder.
" I have captured two stand of arms," said he, with
the air of a conqueror. A clergyman of no very
distinguished ability once received the " semi-lunar
fardels" at a college Commencement. Delighted
with the dignity, he asked President Humphrey,

" On what principle do you confer these titles?"

" We give them," was the reply, " to three classes
of men: First, to those who eminently deserve
them; second, to those whose friends would be
gratified by the honor conferred; third, to those
who cannot possibly get along without them !"

No one ever enjoyed a harmless joke more than
he. No one was more fond of a good story. He
had many College jokes in his *repertoire*, and often
related them. We have often seen him linger, as
he was leaving a room in which his children were
relating the humors of the day, that he might carry

away the flavor of the jest.   Sometimes, when the
joke seemed a little questionable, he would stop
behind the half-closed door until the burst of laughter came, and then go away, his white teeth glisten-
ing along the hall; not quite willing to rebuke, nor
unwilling to enjoy.

His moral sensibilities were predominant.   Chief
among them all was conscience.   In the Mint at
Philadelphia is a delicate machine for testing the
weight of coin.   A quantity of gold-pieces is poured
into a receptacle which opens against the breast of
a wheel.   This wheel is put in revolution.   The
coins pass down the periphery, and are received on
a series of scales, so contrived that if the coins which
fall upon them are below the standard weight, they
are thrown into one compartment below; if above,
into another; if of standard weight, into a third.
Dr. Humphrey's conscience was as sensitive and
discriminating as this machine.   His own thoughts
and acts, as also the thoughts and acts of others,
were incessantly tried by it.   Nothing could induce
him to put a rejected coin in circulation.   We have
already referred to the uneasiness of soul which resulted from a single neglect of public worship, while
a lad, on a day of fasting.   In his papers we find:
" In thinking over my farming days, one reflection
gives me great satisfaction: I never, that I can

recollect, deceived my employers, and never disappointed them if I could help it. When I went home on a visit, I made it a point to return at the time which was set; and I cannot remember that I ever failed." He speaks reproachfully of having, on one occasion, slept an hour among the leaves on a warm April day, when he should have been at work. It was his only offence of this nature. None but a man of sterling conscience would have remembered it so long. He was habitually exact in his dealings with men.

An Amherst merchant has recently told us that Dr. Humphrey invariably threw himself upon the conscience of the dealer in selecting his purchases, and then paid the uttermost farthing. He once purchased a horse of a man who, while accepting the price offered, told him that the animal was worth ten dollars more than the limit his customer had fixed. After trying the animal, Dr. Humphrey was so well satisfied with the purchase that he returned to the dealer and insisted upon his accepting the extra sum. This scrupulous conscientiousness undoubtedly gave its tone to his religious experiences. It was this which in his dying hours made it seem so fearful a thing for a sinner—even a sinner redeemed—to stand before a holy God.

Closely allied to his conscientiousness, was a re-

12 *

markable *humility.* He was not inclined to depre-
ciate his abilities; nor was he ever guilty of over-
estimating them. He never coveted places of
honor; he spontaneously shrank from them, yet
assumed them when it became plain that duty called
him. He was never jealous of other men, though
they were occupying positions which his friends
thought he could better fill. Dr. Todd says of him :

"Humility pervaded his whole character. We
never heard him complain of neglect, hard usage,
or of any disappointment. Even in age, when the
old war-horse could not snuff the battle and laugh
at the rattling of the spear as he once could, he sub-
mitted as quietly and as meekly as a little child who
had never left the shadows of his father's house.
It was not the humility produced by comparing
himself with other men, but humility before God,
learned by leaning against the cross and looking
into the face of Jesus. And when we beheld his
face shining as did the face of Moses, we knew it
was because he had dwelt long in the mount with
God."

His humility was nowhere so conspicuous as in
his estimate of himself as a subject of God's government. "What is man, that thou art mindful of him,
and the son of man, that thou visitest him?" was the
frequent exclamation of his prayer. He looked up

to the great Jehovah with an awful reverence. His "Invocation" in the sanctuary was often as solemn as if he expected the departed glories of the Shekinah to burst again in the house of God.

Associated with his humility was a beautiful simplicity and magnanimity of character. He was as guileless and transparent as a child; as ready to apologize for or to forgive an enemy as if he could not see a bad intention. His friends were sometimes almost impatient with him for his want of what they considered a just resentment. Meanwhile he went forward, subduing by his magnanimity those who perhaps might have only impatiently thrown off the "coals of fire" which resentment kindles. In his simplicity he was often surprised that others should "stand upon etiquette." In his magnanimity he would go far to say a kind word or do a kind act for one who had injured him.

His *benevolence* was large and systematically cultivated. He believed in God's promises to the cheerful giver and to the liberal soul. In his later years, he invariably laid aside a certain proportion of all his pecuniary receipts to enable him to meet the constant calls of charity. Among his papers is a memorandum-book, in which he was in the habit of entering all his income; the smallest fragments, that which was paid for a newspaper article

or a Sunday's preaching among the rest, and
against every entry was a cross, followed by the
fractional sign which indicated the proportion
appropriated to benevolence. The " charity fund"
was generally kept between the leaves of this book.
Hence he almost always had " something to give"
which had already passed into the Lord's treasury.
Thus he always knew how much to appropriate,
and giving was " easy." Sometimes, however, he
would give " upon faith." We have often heard
him relate the story of an impoverished woman,
who, being reduced to the last extremity, declared
to him that she did not know what next to do except
" to begin to give." On one occasion, at least, he
illustrated the theory underlying the poor woman's
remark, by a gift which, on any other theory, would
seem extravagant. The American Board of Com-
missioners for Foreign Missions was near the close
of one of its difficult financial years. A special
appeal was made for funds. It was so urgent that
he felt impelled to contribute a sum which at that
time could not on any system of worldly economics
be spared. " The Lord will provide," said he, as
he gave it. During the following week he received
an invitation to perform a marriage ceremony in a
neighboring town. He complied, and, to his great
surprise, received a fee of exactly the sum con-

tributed. Dr. Humphrey's affections were deep and rich, yet he was not peculiarly demonstrative. The current was even and tranquil, without freshet, without waterfall.

That with these excellences of character some defects were mingled, he, if now living to read this sketch, would be foremost to declare; but no fault in him was ever so clear as the lowest of his virtues. Let us appeal once more to the language of his funeral sermon:

"In speaking of the character of this father, I should fear to express my honest convictions in full among any people who did not know him as you have done. I, certainly, have had good opportunities to read his character, and I may speak with the reverence of a son and the frankness of a friend. And I honestly and deliberately say, that though it would be weak and wicked to call any man perfect, yet *I have never known a man who, in my estimation, came so near being faultless as Dr. Humphrey.* High praise, you will say; and yet there is not a man in this community who would dissent from it."

If the qualities thus delineated are kept in view, we shall carry some light with us in conducting the remainder of our analysis.

THE PREACHER.

It would naturally be supposed that the peculiarities of Dr. Humphrey's early culture would exhibit themselves in his pulpit discourses. To a certain extent they did, at the outset of his ministry. Yet the style of his first sermons was not more defective than that of many a young preacher who has all the educational advantages of the present day. It was, perhaps, somewhat ambitious; yet our teachers now prefer occasional flights by their pupils to a tame and level propriety. A bird will never draw its even circles on the sky without first venturing on irregular wings. What is most observable in the style of Dr. Humphrey's early productions is an intense earnestness and a certain robust quality. The sweep of his sentences was like that of the arm which could reap an acre per day in the harvest-field. The thought is clear and the manner of expression is forcible and vivid. The quotations we have made from his sermons on Temperance, in Fairfield, afford an average example. By practice he gained rapid improvement, and soon became one of the most attractive preachers of his day. Perhaps his power in the pulpit was never so great as during the period covered by the twenty years between 1815 and 1835. His voice was then strong and mellow; his delivery was animated and often powerful. He was frequently invited to preach on important occasions, and seldom disappointed his audience. His eloquence was never stormy, but was often impassioned in a high degree. The cast of his sermons was, for that day, "fresh" and "modern." He emancipated himself from the mechanical divisions and subdivisions, the "improvements" and the interminable vertebræ of inference, so much employed by celebrated preachers before him. Not that he wrote without a "plan;" not that he rejected the numerals and the "heads" which they designated; but that he made his divisions so few and so natural that the articulations of his "skeletons" were not painfully apparent. He sought the advantage of freshness in his preaching, so far as it could be made promotive of true power. He would sacrifice nothing to effect; he would make use of effect so far as it might aid him in promoting the triumphs of the Gospel.

He was never "sensational" in the pulpit. He never there indulged in wit or sarcasm—scarcely ever in the mildest humor. His strain was always dignified and lofty. One would say that in his ordinary ministrations he was rather a "legal" than a "spiritual" preacher—that is, in this modified sense, that he dwelt much upon the governmental as closely associated with the redemptive aspects of Christianity. He had no confidence in " works." Faith was to him the one condition of eternal life; yet he stoutly proclaimed God a Sovereign, and man a rebel under infinite obligations to repent and submit to a rejected authority. He centred all his hopes and all the hopes of the world upon the Cross; yet the life of obedience was made, perhaps, more prominent than the life which is fed in conscious union with Christ. He preached the hard doctrines, stripping bare the heart in its depravity, then throwing it back on the mercy of Him whose " strong decrees" already enclose the destiny of every man. Christ was to him a Sovereign Redeemer, rather than a personal intimate for every man's heart and home.

The results of his preaching were eminently " spiritual." He aimed to secure that obedience which springs spontaneously from a sanctified heart. The piety he loved was thoroughly experimental. One of his favorite books was " Edwards on the Affections." He had no confidence in a piety based upon a simple act of submission to God and a resolution to live a holy life. Regeneration and sanctification by the Holy Ghost were central ideas in his creed. His presentation of the hard doctrines was designed to promote an absolute dependence upon the Triune God as Sovereign, as Sanctifier and as Redeemer. He was satisfied with nothing less than a rectification of the affections as well as of the will. In these respects, as well as in many others, he was representative of the period over which his life was spread. When the type of popular preaching was so far changed as to bring man's responsibility into the foreground, he was not slow to recognize the usefulness of this mode of address. He sought to blend the advantages of the earlier and of the later type, so as to avail himself of both.

" However paradoxical it may seem," he writes in his autobiographical papers, " I am persuaded that sinners ought to be just as earnestly exhorted to give their hearts immediately to God as if no divine help were needed; for there is nothing in the way but their own desperate depravity. On the other hand, the agency of the Holy Spirit in turning men from darkness to light ought to be kept as distinctly in view as if no other agency were concerned in the matter; for no sinner ever will come to Christ except the Father draw him. There is no way to deprive him of all his excuses, and make him despair of helping himself, but by preaching free agency and entire dependence upon the sovereign mercy of God."

His exalted idea of the preacher's office is well

13   K

exhibited by a passage from a sermon delivered before the Annual Convention of the Congregational Ministers of Massachusetts, in Boston, May 29, 1830:

"Never, surely, were duties so momentous devolved by any temporal prince upon his most confidential servants as those which devolve upon every minister of Christ. Never were such mighty interests suspended upon a single word or action. Never, in the proudest days of Assyrian or Persian glory, did those who stood nearest the throne act under such amazing responsibility. Never were such rewards promised to good and faithful servants. Think, oh think, of the unspeakable difference! A minister of State may, by his wisdom and fidelity, gain a new province for his master, or may lose half the kingdom by his treachery or neglect. An ambassador may, by a skillful and timely negotiation, dissipate or turn away the gathering storm of war from his country; or he may so misrepresent his sovereign in a foreign court as to darken the political heavens at once and bring down the tempest in all its fury. For his fidelity and success he may be rewarded with domains or titles, or, if unfaithful to his high trust, he may be banished or beheaded for his crime. But weigh these interests, these rewards, these penalties, if you can, against the interests of the kingdom of Christ; the worth of the undying soul; the smiles, or the wrath of the Lamb; the heights of ' glory and honor and immortality,' or the unfathomable depths of shame and remorse and agony! Time here, and eternity there! A feather in one scale, and the everlasting mountains in the other!"

His views of the glory of Christ's kingdom are also presented in the same discourse. Redemption, to him, meant the subjection of a world to him whose right it is to rule and reign, King of nations as he is King of saints.

"How glorious is the kingdom of Christ, in its constitution, in its laws, in its administration, and in its peaceful advance to universal empire! Every great movement, every new conquest, every trophy reminds us that it is not of this world. Its all-pervading spirit is the spirit of holiness, of love, of pure disinterested benevolence. While the factitious glare of earthly monarchies conceals a vast amount of corruption, misery and crime under an imposing exterior, the kingdom of Immanuel ' is all glorious within;' and the emanations of this central glory will shine ' more and more unto the perfect day.' As in the natural world the empire of the sun advances just as fast and as far as the light shines, so it is with the Sun of Righteousness. His dominion will become universal, just as soon as he shall irradiate all lands. Behold, then, how his celestial beams already gild the spires of ten thousand temples dedicated to his worship! See how fast the light wings its way from one dark mountain to another. See how the shadows of death flee before it, as it glances upon the pagoda and the mosque; as it shines broadly upon the islands of the Pacific and penetrates the savage wilderness of our own country. Extend your view still farther. See every great valley of death illumined, every moral desert reclaimed, every foul spirit cast out, every pagan altar thrown down, every nation and every tribe under heaven coming joyfully under the peaceful sceptre of Jesus! Then listen to ' numbers without number' of jubilant voices in every variety of human language hymning praises to the Redeemer!"

Among the favorite sermons which he loved to preach in the evening of life, were two, one of which is upon the text, " On his head were many crowns." Rev. xix. 13. It presents a glowing picture of the glory of Christ, as he shall appear when all things shall have been placed under his feet.

The other embodies the anticipations of one who has devoted many long years to a study which, however profound, can carry one but little beyond the alphabet in this mortal state. He felt, with Sir Isaac

Newton, that he had been like a child gathering shells on the beach of an unexplored sea. He looked forward with longing to the experiences of that period when the sea itself should be traversed and sounded. The text of this sermon is, Col. i. 9, 10. Its key-words are those already quoted as cut upon his monument, so vividly expressive of what he has already begun to realize—"*Increasing in the knowledge of God.*" On the cover of the manuscript is written the title; a record of the pulpits in which the discourse was preached—twenty-seven in all; also the first lines of several appropriate hymns, such as:

" Lord, when my raptured thought surveys !"

" Great God, how infinite art thou !"

" Come, O my soul, in sacred lays !"

" My God ! my portion and my love !"

Its style of thought and expression may be inferred from the following passages taken from near the close:

" We have as much evidence that the saints in light will increase in the knowledge of God, as that their happiness will increase; for happiness and knowledge in the world of glory are inseparable. The more they know of God the more they will love him; and the more they love him the happier will they be. The human soul is made for

13 *

progress. It thirsts for knowledge; and though a depraved heart weakens and obscures the intellect, still, when knowable objects are presented to the mind, it will learn something; how much more, when, renewed, washed and perfectly sanctified, it enters heaven, and all its glories break upon the enraptured vision! There may be latent energies in the soul of man which will astonish angels when they come to be developed. We know that the human mind is essentially spiritual and active. There is no proof that it ever sleeps a single hour from infancy to old age. Nor, after it leaves the body and gets the free use of its wings, have we reason to think it ever tires.

" Think of the countless millions of suns and systems which astronomy has already revealed to mortal vision. Who can tell how many of these the redeemed will visit, or what discoveries they will make of God's ineffable glory beyond what hath entered into the heart of man? And then, beyond all these stars and the nebulæ yet unresolved, there is room enough in the infinite depths of space for millions of other suns and systems to one that has yet been discovered. Who can tell how many millions of them the saints will be permitted to visit in the progress of everlasting ages, or what new displays of God's power and glory they will witness in

each of them? Oh, what a mighty range, what a
vast duration, what advantages for increasing in the
knowledge of God; of studying his adorable character in the garnished heavens, and through the
endless cycles of his governmental rule! But that
which the redeemed will study with the most intense
interest; that which will ravish their souls beyond
all other knowledge, is the great mystery of godliness—God manifest in the flesh. Whatever else
may occupy their minds, this theme will ever be
uppermost. The glory of Christ will eclipse all
other glories. The knowledge of God in Christ
will, as it were, swallow up all other knowledge.
Wherever sent, in whatever ministrations employed,
their thoughts will not for a moment be withdrawn
from him.

"And if, as we have reason to believe, other
worlds and orders of beings are, in ways unknown
to us, deeply interested in the work of redemption,
how much wider views may be opened to the adoring contemplation of the general assembly and
Church of the first-born! We can hardly suppose
that angels and men are the only beings in the
universe who desire to look into this mystery of
mysteries. Moreover, who can tell but that God
has yet other attributes to display to an admiring
universe beside those which have been already un-

folded? His justice and mercy were both kept concealed from eternity till the fall of angels and men brought them out; and I ask again, who can tell what other attributes may be disclosed to an adoring universe as eternal ages roll on? Oh, what unspeakable advantages will the righteous enjoy for increasing in the knowledge of God as long as God himself shall exist to irradiate the universe with his glory! How will their faculties expand as the ineffable brightness is poured in upon their minds! how fast will they increase in the knowledge of God! how will their hearts glow with love! with what ecstasy, as they rise from glory to glory through everlasting ages, will they shout, ' Unto Him that loved us and washed us from our sins in his own blood, and hath made us kings and priests unto God and his Father, to him be glory and dominion for ever and ever! Amen.' Oh, how will they make the arches ring with their hallelujahs! Why cannot *we* hear the celestial chorus? We shall hear it and join in the innumerable throng before the throne of God and the Lamb, if we are washed in the same atoning blood."

What thoughts are these to carry with one through the sunset, whose fading glories may well be left behind without a sigh!

In thus describing Dr. Humphrey as a preacher,

we have rendered it unnecessary to speak of him as a theologian. He was deeply interested in all the theological controversies of the time. How notable and how warm those controversies were, will appear to any one who recalls the Unitarian discussion whose centre was Boston, and whose principal champions on the side of Orthodoxy were Dr. Griffin, Dr. Lyman Beecher and Dr. Leonard Woods; the New Haven controversy which centred about Dr. N. W. Taylor; and the discussion occasioned by the revival movements of Dr. Nettleton on the one side, and Pres. Finney on the other. In these controversies Dr. Humphrey played no mean part. On what side his lance was couched may be gathered from our statement of his views. The conflicts are now over; their dust is blown out of the horizon; most of their principal contestants are gone where men see eye to eye. Their results indeed remain, but we will not attempt to record the history of the struggle.

THE EDUCATOR.

Wide and deep as was Dr. Humphrey's influence in the pulpit, the great work of his life was that of the educator. We have seen how the tastes formed in the obscure school districts of his native county abode with him, impelled him to the teacher's work

while in college, led him to interest himself in the
public schools of his two parishes, and finally obtained their full development and exercise in the
office of President.   The theme of education in the
home, in the school, in the academy, in the college,
was ever present in his mind.   He wrote many
sermons on the subject.   He delivered many ad
dresses in State and County Educational Conventions.   The atmosphere of such conventions was
congenial to his spirit.   While breathing it, old
memories were sure to wake, and his thoughts were
ever near his lips.   Very touching are these words
from the opening of an address before a Convention
of Teachers, held in Hartford, November 10, 1830:

"I congratulate myself on being permitted this day
to meet, and to exchange salutations with so many
zealous and enlightened friends of education from
every part of Connecticut.   And it greatly heightens
the pleasure of these greetings that I appear among
you, not as a stranger, but as a native-born citizen.
You will believe me when I say that the objects of
this convention and the presence of early friends
and associates, awaken in my breast recollections
and feelings which I love to cherish.

" Memory, that mysterious chronicler of bygone
years, carries me back with the swiftness of thought
to the period when the ' dew of youth' lay fresh

upon my buoyant spirits; and when, in a humbler sphere, I first assumed the responsibilities of a school-master. Time and space for a moment seem to be annihilated. I am again in the very house where first I met the bright and inquisitive glance of twenty scholars. I look out, and the same snow covers the hills. I look up, and the same winter clouds are hurrying through the skies. I listen again, as I did thirty years ago, to the oracular voices of old and experienced teachers; and I feel again the stirring of the same young enthusiasm which then glowed in my bosom. I forget that with me the warm spring of life is so long past, and ·that autumn is even now sprinkling its flakes upon a spot so bleak that it cannot retain them. Those fine chords so long untouched, which once bound the heart to the village-school, again vibrate and pour their harmony into its secret audience, bringing me into near and delightful fellowship with all the friends of popular education throughout the land."

Of his ideas as an educator but little need be said to those who have read the foregoing pages. Christianity was the base and the animating principle of them all. He would educate the country for the sake of Christ and of the world.

When he assumed the Presidency of Amherst College, he felt that if profound and varied learning were the great requisite, then he was unfitted for the post. But he saw that something more than this was needed; and he dared not resist the verdict which decided that he was the choice of Providence. How he struggled in fulfilling his duties, how he succeeded, we have already told. Let another witness speak in words stronger than we have ventured to use. Again we quote from the funeral sermon:

"Few men could, or would have toiled on, year after year, as he did. Slowly the walls went up—as did the walls of Jerusalem under Nehemiah; and after a toil of twenty-two years—a toil that seldom has a parallel—and without stopping an hour, save once to hasten across the Atlantic when worn down and ready to perish, he came to the place where he must stop. Loving labor more than food, and loving his College with the love of a father, he saw that it was the will of God that he should now lay down the burden and retire. It then seemed as if he could never rally, and that he must die soon. What had he done? He had gathered around him a noble Faculty of teachers; he had raised new buildings as fast as needed; he had gathered around the College the confidence and the sympathy of the Christian community; he had gathered funds and friends that would sustain the institution in full vigor; he had placed it among the brightest luminaries of the land; he had got it incorporated and made it to be respected; he had superintended the education and seen graduate under his own eye 795 young men, sent out to leave their mark upon the world, of whom 430 he saw become ministers of the gospel, and of these 84 are numbered as pastors in Massachusetts at this hour, and 39 were sent abroad as missionaries of the cross. Sixty-eight of these young ministers have passed away, and were on the other side of the river to welcome their beloved instructor. Some of them were bright and shining lights. He, being dead, yet liveth and speaketh through all these—and they, to tens of thousands—and onward and downward the influences roll to the end of time. What the results are and will be in this world, no tongue can tell; nor will they cease for ever. The hallowed influences which have been impressed upon other minds and hearts are so many cords of love and mercy which remain to draw souls to Christ. And many a poor boy, and many a poor schoolmaster, will grow strong and be lighted up in hope and courage, as he tries to prepare himself for usefulness, by knowing that the great and the good Heman Humphrey was once a poor boy and a poor schoolmaster, urging his way up to one of the highest posts of usefulness in the land!"

14

Had he accomplished no other work than this, he would have gone down to an honored grave.

He never lost his interest in the College. He had loved the faithful instructors who wrought with him in his work, he had loved the very walls of the buildings which grew up under his administration. He delighted in nothing more than to revisit the institution, to review the past with those who had been his fellow-workers, and to congratulate his successors upon the prosperity of the College under their hands. He was grateful for the cordiality with which he was always received, and never ceased to pray for and to rejoice in the growth of the institution.

Much might be said of the influence he exerted in moulding the Common-school system of Massachusetts. He believed that the college sent some of its roots down into the common schools; and for its sake he would have these lower seminaries as perfect as possible; for its sake he manfully contended for the use of the Bible in those schools when a persistent effort was made to exclude it; for the sake of the college, but not less for the sake of the State and of the Land.

THE PHILANTHROPIST.

Dr. Humphrey wrote high on his list of maxims that old Latin sentiment, *Homo sum*, etc. He was in the highest sense a humanitarian; not the less, but the more, because he held so tenaciously to an orthodox theology. No mistake is greater than that a man must cease to care for the temporal interests of his fellows in proportion as he seeks the salvation of their souls. His labors in behalf of temperance were not intermitted until the temperance reformation was fully established. One of his most vigorous discourses was an address, delivered to the students of Amherst College, July 4, 1828, the subject being a Parallel between Intemperance and the Slave Trade. This address was printed, attained a wide circulation, and—like Dr. Marsh's " Putman and the Wolf"—was extensively useful.

His sympathy for the slave was quick and strong. He was never an Abolitionist, in the technical sense of that term. He fully believed, up to the period of the civil war, that the American Colonization Society presented the most hopeful means for the mitigation, and perhaps for the ultimate removal, of the blight and the wrongs of American slavery. Yet, while recognizing the constitutional difficulties which embarrassed political action in this matter, he looked with favor upon all schemes which promised a gradual emancipation. He strenuously opposed all extension of the area of slavery by governmental action. When, in 1854, the "Missouri Compromise," which declared that from all territory " purchased of France, lying north of 36 deg. 30 min., slavery and involuntary servitude, otherwise than in the punishment of crimes, shall be, and is hereby for ever prohibited," was threatened by the "Nebraska Bill," his blood was stirred. He delivered an address on the subject before the citizens of Pittsfield, in the Baptist Church, on Sunday evening, February 26, which was characterized by all his youthful fire. The repeal of this Compromise seemed to him so gross a violation of the public faith, that he could not restrain his indignant protest. It was to him like one of the vital questions of the Revolution. And, as the ministers of 1776 were impelled to speak, so he thought those of 1854 should keep not silence.

"What if," said he in his sermon, "that venerable man of God, Rev. Thomas Allen, who sleeps in yonder tomb, could be waked up, and have the Nebraska Bill with its black section put into his hand—what would HE say? I declare to you, I would not for any price go and knock at the door of that tomb, if I knew that I would bring him up, except it were in the last extremity of expiring liberty, that he might again buckle on his armor and march up to the cannon's mouth. No; let him sleep, and never till the day of judgment know anything of the atrocious conspiracy which has been concocted this winter at the seat of Government!"

It is well known that the Nebraska Bill was among the beginnings of the end; that, in the providence of God, the whole question of slavery was solved by the war which in a few years followed; that Mr. Douglas himself, the great advocate of the repeal of the Compromise, became one of the instruments by which the power and the existence of slavery were for ever destroyed in the United States. The burning words which Dr. Humphrey again poured out in Pittsfield when the first gun had been fired upon Fort Sumter were those of one who loved his country, and hated that system which, through the precipitancy of its advocates, was hastening to its end.

The same feeling which made him the friend of the slave, made him the friend of all the oppressed. In 1829 he delivered an address in Amherst, Hartford, and other places, on "Indian Rights and our Duties." It was occasioned by the forcible expulsion of the Indians, "in violation of a score of treaties," to the western bank of the Mississippi.

14 *   • L

"I could not help remonstrating with all the power I had. I said then, and I say now, that I would rather receive the blessing of one poor Indian, as he looks back for the last time on the graves of his fathers, than to sleep under the marble of all the Cæsars."

He was also an early and an enthusiastic supporter of Christian Missions. He enjoyed the honor of preaching the sermon at the ordination of the first missionaries of the A. B. C. F. M. to the Sandwich Islands—Rev. Hiram Bingham and Rev. Asa Thurston. The service was held at Goshen, Connecticut, September 29, 1819. He was identified with almost every prominent organization in his day for the spread of the Gospel. He was interested in Asylums and Retreats for the unfortunate. He sought the mitigation of unnecessary discipline in Prisons and Penitentiaries. A sermon preached in Pittsfield, on the day of the Annual Fast, April 4, 1818, upon "Doing Good to the Poor," shows how great his compassion for this class of society whom "we have ever with us," and how just his discrimination in affording them a needed relief.

THE AUTHOR.

Dr. Humphrey wielded a facile and unwearied pen. From the time when the educational essays of *Lictor* appeared in a New Haven journal, he made frequent use of the press. After the struggles incident to the founding of Amherst College were over, he was in almost constant communication with the public, by type as well as by tongue. His style as a writer was simple and direct. " First clearness, then force," was his maxim. His sentences were like crystal lenses rather than like pictured windows. Yet, when occasion served, he was graphic in description or eloquent in thought. His writings commended themselves, however, more by the ideas they conveyed than by the rhetoric with which they were adorned. Some one compares the style of John Foster to " a lumbering wagon filled with gold." The comparison would not describe the style of Dr. Humphrey, even in his more negligent moods. Yet it may be truly said that he was more solicitous to have the gold in the vehicle than to have the vehicle itself highly ornamented. It would not be difficult, nevertheless, to fill many pages with extracts whose rhetoric is as pure as their thought is valuable. As a writer for newspapers, he was among the most popular of the day. Probably no letters from abroad have ever been more widely read than those which he published in the *New York Observer.* His " Letters to a Son in the Ministry," first issued in the columns of a religious journal, were perused almost as eagerly by the occupants of the pew as by the occupants of the pulpit. His "Revival Conversations," appearing first in the *New England Puritan*, were read with universal interest and profit. The demand for each of these serial issues was only satisfied by their collection in permanent form. The same also may be said of his "Letters on Domestic Education." His miscellaneous contributions to the periodical press would fill many volumes. What he wrote may not go into the permanent literature of the land, except by indirection. It was enough for him to reach and influence the minds of thousands while he lived.

Among the most important of his published sermons and addresses are—

1. Sermon before the Moral Society of Connecticut.　New Haven, 1815.

2. Sermon "On Doing Good to the Poor." Pittsfield, 1818.

3. Sermon before the Berkshire County Education Society.　Lenox, 1818.

4. Sermon at the Ordination of the Missionaries destined to the Sandwich Islands.　Boston, 1819.

5. Address commemorative of the Landing of the Pilgrims.　Pittsfield, 1820.　Second Centennial Anniversary.

6. Address at his Inauguration as President. Amherst, 1823.

7. Sermon before the Pastoral Association of Massachusetts. "The Good Pastor." Boston, 1826.

8. Sermon at the Dedication of the Chapel at Amherst College, 1827.

9. Address. "Parallel between Intemperance and the Slave Trade." Amherst, 1828.

10. Sermon on "Indian Rights and our Duties." Amherst, 1829.

11. Massachusetts Convention Sermon. "The Kingdom of Christ." Boston, 1830.

12. Address before Teachers' Convention. Hartford, 1830.

13. Sermon before the American Sunday-School Union. Philadelphia, 1831.

14. Sermon at the Funeral of Nathaniel Smith, Esq., of Sunderland. "The Good Arimathean." Amherst, 1833.

15. Sermon before the Students of Amherst College. "A Glorious Enterprise." Amherst, 1834.

16. Sermon on the Sixth Commandment. "Dueling." Amherst, 1838.

17. The Bible in Public Schools. "American Institute." 1843.

18. Valedictory Address on leaving the Presidency. Amherst, 1845.

19. Address at the opening of a Normal School-house, Westfield, Massachusetts.   Boston, 1846.

20. Tribute to the Memory of Rev. Nathan W. Fiske, Professor.   Amherst, 1848.

21. Sermon at the Funeral of Miss Mary Lyon, South Hadley.   "The Shining Path."   Northampton, 1849.

22. "The Missouri Compromise."   Pittsfield, 1854.

23. Sermon on the Day of National Fast.   Pittsfield, 1861.

His published works, in volumes, are :

1. Prize Essays on the Sabbath.   1830.

2. Miscellaneous Discourses and Reviews.   1834.

3. Christian Memoirs.   1836.

4. Tour in France, Great Britain and Belgium, 2 vols.   1838.

5. Domestic Education.   1840.

6. Revival Conversations.   1844.

7. Letters to a Son in the Ministry.   1845.

8. Life and Writings of Prof. N. W. Fiske. 1850.

9. Life and Writings of Rev. T. H. Gallaudet. 1857.

10. Sketches of the History of Revivals.   1859.

He also wrote numerous articles for Religious Reviews and monthly periodicals.   His earlier papers of this description appeared in the *Panoplist* and the *Christian Spectator.*

"As an author," says Dr. Sprague, "he has commanded high respect on both sides of the Atlantic; his works are all characterized by that sobriety, transparency and richness of thought, and that simplicity and purity of style, that are fitted to secure for them an enduring posthumous usefulness."

To render our analysis complete, we should speak of Dr. Humphrey in his domestic relations and in his character as a friend. Let it suffice to say, that he was as evenly balanced in his most private life as in the recitation-room, the pulpit or the ecclesiastical council. His "unbending" was never so absolute as that of some strong natures; but especially in the twenty last years of his life, he was a most genial companion in the household or in general society. A popular preacher discourses upon the different shadows men cast. Acts v. 15. Dr. Humphrey's shadow was always pleasant, and oftentimes a soothing one, if not, like St. Peter's, full of healing. "Shadow" is another term for what is sometimes described as "atmosphere." Dr. Humphrey's atmosphere was warm, yet brisk. If it was not as full of magnetic attractions as that of some men, it was not as full of repulsions as that of some others.

Every one, in fact, enjoyed his society. The stranger found, in a little while, that Dr. Humphrey had numerous points of contact with all about him. If he was never so young as to be charged with foolishness, he was never so old as to be out of sympathy with those of freshest life. He became more and more genial with advancing years. To visit his children and to gather them and their children about him was one of his highest pleasures.

His family was large, but had been many times broken in upon by death. Our parents had ten children. Edward, James, Sophia and John, were born in Fairfield; Lucy, the first Mary, and Henry Martin, in Fairfield; Zephaniah, the second Mary, and Sarah, in Amherst. But four of the ten are now surviving. The first Mary, Sophia and Henry, were buried in Amherst. John sleeps in Pittsfield, James in Brooklyn, and Mary in Honesdale, Pennsylvania.

The dying sire has left behind him no ancestral wealth, but he carried with him into the other world that which " cannot be gotten for gold, neither shall silver be weighed for the price thereof." He has left none of the reputation of a great discoverer, but he learned that of which " the depth saith, It is not in me; and the sea saith, It is not in me." His choicest bequest to us is that " good name which is rather to be chosen than great riches," and that memory of the just which is blessed.

Z. M. H.

PHILADELPHIA, *April*, 1869.
15

Mrs. Sophia Humphrey.

MRS. SOPHIA HUMPHREY.

AT the close of one of the bright days of the month of October, 1807, a young lady could be seen in the town of Farmington, Connecticut, standing at the front door of the house adjoining that now occupied by the wife and daughters of the late Rev. Noah Porter; and looking, as she wrote in one of her letters, at " the serene and solemn beauty displayed in the Creator's works."

There is reason to believe that the quality which on that evening revealed itself to her with unwonted vividness, as investing the objects of Nature, had for many years dwelt in every chamber of her mind, and even given attractiveness to her person. Her form was one of unusual symmetry. She was tall, erect, well-proportioned. Her movement was graceful, and had withal a gentle dignity. The features of her face, with only a glimmer however of their pleasing expression, can still be seen in the photo-

15 *   173

graphs you have, taken when she was about seventy-six years of age. This young lady was Miss Sophia Porter, the daughter of Noah and Rachel Merrill Porter, "the descendants of ancestors who had lived in the Farmington Valley since 1652." Mr. Porter had recently sold his farm and landed estate, and purchased a house in the village, and moved into it, that he might pass his remaining years with not less usefulness, and in more tranquil enjoyment of the mercies which God had conferred upon him. He had three sons and two daughters: Edward, a minister and teacher; Robert, a judge in New York; and Noah, for sixty years the minister of Farmington. The second daughter and youngest child was your grandmother, born December 27, 1785. And it is from her diary and compositions written at school, and from her letters to her friends and to Mr. Heman Humphrey, then a young minister at Fairfield, that we get the first glimpse of the disinterested nature, the tender affection, the scrupulous integrity, the discerning and well-balanced mind, and the desire to honor God, which characterized her entire life.

None who knew your grandmother had ever a doubt that, whatever it was that prompted her constant and sustained activity, it was nothing that terminated upon herself. She never thought of

herself. And it was this self-obliviousness that gave
that charming simplicity and grace to her manners,
and that real affectionateness to her heart, which
distinguished her. Endowed with what would be
called in these days a vigorous intellect and a
sound judgment, yet she never regarded these as
worthy of taking the leading place in the conduct
of her social, domestic or religious life. In a letter
written to a very dear friend, in December, 1807,
about three months before her marriage, she says,
after alluding to the conflict between the Rev. John
Newton's head and heart, "I have also a controversy between my head and heart, or at least they
are each of them determined to take all the merit to
themselves. Head insists that the perpetuity of
affection depends entirely on the observance of external duties; and of course that these must be the
foundation of happiness. This I think is plausible.
On the other hand, heart is decided in the opinion
that duty will be more strictly performed, and happiness better insured, by a conduct influenced by
real disinterested affection, than that constrained
by any set of rules."

The sentiment expressed in these lines took such
possession of her in the bloom of life that it never
left her. To every minor act of her after days it
gave direction and beauty. Whether in bidding wel-

come to a stranger, or in preparing for a guest
what her husband called in patriarchal language
" savory meat," that same desire to make some
one a little happier animated her face and moved
her hand.   Neither age, nor deafness, nor change
of place, could diminish the strength of this habit of
mind.   What came forth in the letters and glowed
in the heart of the maiden at Farmington, and
burned as a flame at Fairfield, lost none of
its intensity at Pittsfield or at Amherst.   Widening
the sphere of her usefulness could neither diminish
the strength nor alloy the quality of her self-abnegating spirit.   After her return to Pittsfield,
although the almond tree had begun to blossom,
and her years were approaching fourscore and
three, the passion of her heart still lived and
wrought, " burning brightly amidst the frosts of
age."   Even during her last sickness, in her days
of extreme weakness, when not only the silver cord
began to loosen, but the golden bowl to break, she
did not cease, to inquire after the comfort of whatever had been near her.   "Have you fed the bird?"
she would say, as one daughter looked into her face.
"I was afraid you had not."   "Have you kept anything for her?" as she thought of her grandchild re-
turning from school.   And on the very last day of
her life, when every sound was brought low unto

sobbing, she would place her hand in those of her daughters and say, " Take care of yourselves, don't mind me."

This forgetfulness of herself made her value at far less than their real worth her own powers and acquisitions. Whilst she never ceased to exercise her rare capacity for discriminating between the false and the true, the superficial and the substantial; and did not hesitate to express, in remarkably appropriate phrase, her opinion when asked for it; yet when in the presence of any who occupied or claimed positions of usefulness, she was disposed to sit at their feet.

She not only did not assume anything, but she was pained at receiving the marks of deference involuntarily manifested toward her. " You need a word of caution," she wrote to one whose regard for her was profound; " do not rate me too highly; I fear you will be disappointed." Thus was she at the beginning of life, and thus at the end. This desire not to be overvalued made her perfectly transparent. She could not affect anything. She shrank from exaggeration as from a falsehood. When addressed in words of admiration she would write, " I cannot consider these words as addressed to me, as I am by no means deserving of the appellations. Convinced as I am that adulation was not

M

your design, yet so far as an expression has this appearance, so far it will never be pleasing to your friend."

Do not think, however, that because of this indisposition to press her personality out and make it felt, that she was without character. Far from it. Every step she took, every plan she formed, every child she encouraged, every beggar she relieved, every sick person she remembered, every storekeeper with whom she dealt, can attest that under that quiet and genial face, and within that unobtrusive form, there dwelt deep feeling and outspoken honesty. No emotion of her nature was cold. She could become impassioned when off her guard; nor was she always unwilling to let persons know that they must not attempt to impose upon her. For her husband and her children she laid out her strength and thoughts with a prodigality ceaseless and unmeasured. She could not do too much for them, and found ample reward in her freely-given toil and their love. Had it not been for her inborn soundness of judgment, she would have erred on the side of an unrestrained abandonment of herself to the comfort of her family. But her regard for their usefulness and her instinctive good sense would not let her forget that to be right is more than to be happy. And her reason came to the help of her

energy and love, and thus she did for them the most
that she could, temporally and spiritually. And in
the circumstances in which she was placed at Fairfield, at Pittsfield and at Amherst, this was no light
task. To shield ten children from temptation, to
foster in them elevated aspirations, to constrain them
to industry, and to keep the wolf from barking too
loudly at the door, required no little administrative
talent and skill. And yet, by reason of her husband's necessary absorption in public labors, these
burdens she took upon herself and carried them
cheerfully. Neither as a mother, nor as a parish-
minister's wife, nor as the sympathizing friend of
young men, nor in the entertainment of strangers,
especially during those twenty-three years that the
College occupied her thoughts and those of your
grandfather, did she fail nobly to do her part.
Common as it may be to quote the words spoken to
King Lemuel, "She riseth up while it is yet night,
and giveth meat to her household. She girdeth her
loins with strength, and strengtheneth her arms.
Her candle goeth not out by night; she stretcheth
out her hand to the poor, yea she reacheth forth her
hands to the needy. Strength and honor are her
clothing; and she shall rejoice in time to come. She
openeth her mouth with wisdom, and in her tongue
is the law of kindness;" yet who can read this de-

scription without thinking of her whose "children now rise up and call her blessed?" No one ever doubted that your grandmother had intellect, and a great deal of it, and that it showed itself in the places where it was most desirable that it should appear—in her daily life and in the management of her affairs. Nor was she without education—a good education, in the technical sense of the word. Her father, whose circumstances were never straitened, and who was himself fond of books, placed her during her childhood at the best schools which were to be found in the neighborhood, and at the age of fifteen sent her from home to a superior seminary under the supervision of her brother Edward, a man of learning who had relinquished the clerical profession in consequence of failing health and the loss of his voice. The journal which she kept at this Academy is still with us, and has in it her compositions, her abstracts of the sermons preached at the church on Sunday, and such remarks on attire, society, and nature, as a young girl might be expected to make. "Asked permission on Sunday to curl my hair; had a repulse; felt a little mortified; did not lay it to heart however," appears on the first page. The exercise on manners enforced once a week, occasions many piquant remarks. Her observations on some of the young gentlemen to whom she was introduced, are also made with much naïveté and freedom. She does not forget to write of Mr. B.: "By attempting to be witty he became very foolish, and even descended to sauciness." The books which formed part of her reading during the period (which was not very long) covered by her journal, were Miss Hannah More's Works, Newton's Letters, Volney's Travels and the History of Paul and Virginia. On Sunday she entertained herself with the Theological Magazine, consisting of essays and sacred poetry. She also read and studied the Bible, and committed to memory the Westminster Assembly's Catechism.

If you would like to see one of her compositions, here is a part of that on the "Critic's Vocation:"

"True criticism is the application of taste and good sense to the fine arts. The object which it proposes is, to distinguish between what is beautiful and what is not. Critics who judge by rule, not by feeling, are pedants, not critics. Even though the public may praise, true criticism may often with reason condemn.

"Taste and genius are different things. Taste is the power to judge, genius to execute. One may have a degree of taste for the fine arts who has hardly any genius for composition, or for executing those arts. But genius cannot be found without in-

16

cluding taste.   Genius therefore deserves to be considered as a higher power of the mind than taste.
Genius always implies something inventive or cre-
ative; but taste rests in mere sensibility to beauty
when it is perceived.   Refined taste makes a good
critic, but genius is necessary for a poet or orator.
Genius is a talent or aptitude which we receive from
nature for excelling in any one thing."   These
points she afterward illustrates.

After thus receiving instruction at the seminary at
Waterbury, and at Clinton, N. Y., she returned to
her father's house, about eighteen years of age;
there she enjoyed the society of her parents, and
that also of her brother Noah, who was four years
older than herself, a graduate of Yale College, the
valedictorian of his class, and at that time studying
for the ministry.   With this brother she had much
intimacy of intercourse and much congeniality of
spirit.   They confided to each other their most
sacred purposes and feelings.   They wrote on similar subjects.   But for this friendship, begun in
childhood and growing closer and more precious
every year, and her deep sympathy with him in his
pursuits, you would be surprised to learn that she
composed and wrote a number of essays on theological themes.   They were on such subjects as
The Being of God, and how to Glorify Him; on the

Divinity of Christ; Justification by Faith; Atonement; Regeneration, etc. Nor can it be supposed that the intimacy between this sister and brother was diminished at all by the fact that, as not far from this time Mr. Heman Humphrey found that "the town of Farmington had many charms," especially that portion of it which contained your great grandfather's house; so, her brother was beginning to discern that the city of Middletown was not without its attractions. Such was the effect of one of its habitations and what it contained on the young Farmington divine, that he is constrained to write to his sister in the month of May, and aver how " heartily pleased" he is with Miss " Hetty Meigs."

Therefore, we say that under the influence and teaching of good schools, intelligent society, and well-instructed divines, old and young, your grandmother was not without some knowledge of the way to put out her thoughts and her feelings.

I will insert here two of her letters which I have selected, not because they fairly represent her epistolary gifts, which were really remarkable, but because of the long interval between them—the one having been written in the early morning and the other late in the evening of her life. The first is dated December 7, 1795, when she was ten years of age (this is given without correction), and the last was written when she was nearly eighty-three years old, November 13, 1868, after the death of her grandson, James Humphrey, Jr., and only four weeks before her own decease. These were her latest written words.

FARMINGTON, *Dec.* 7, 1795.

DEAR BROTHER:

I am pleased that you have not forgotten me in your absence from home, but have sent me an agreable letter full of brotherly advise, which I intend to mind; and, indeed, I find no difficulty in attending to that part of your advise with respect to Mr. Wardsworth,* for I find him very agreable. I think that I learn to wright very fast, but I fear you will have reason to think otherwais when you se this letter. I find that we shall miss you at our school, for the boys have almost cut to pieces that pegg that you made in the door to keep out the cold, and we want you to make another. But I hope you will be able to shew your kind offices in that school as well as here. I shall hope for another letter from you. I shall improve every opportunity to express my regards for you.

Mr. Noah Porter.

* Her teacher.

PITTSFIELD, *Nov.* 13, 1868.

MY VERY DEAR URANIA:

You may be assured that you and yours have been much in my thoughts in all James' long and painful sickness. And now that he is gone, I would express my sorrow and sympathy for your sore bereavement, though beyond my feeble words. I feel devoutly thankful that our sorrow is so far relieved by the consolation and hope that he is now in rest, rejoicing in the glory of God.

Most of our family have gone before us; but thanks to a merciful God we may trust that they are rejoicing together in the heavenly world. . . . . I thank you for the paper sent to me giving an account of the funeral, and something of James' character and religious experience. This was quite satisfactory and comforting. My health and strength I think are slowly failing. I want very much to see you and your dear family. . . . . With much love and sympathy for you all, I am

Your loving mother,

SOPHIA HUMPHREY.

Thus far we have said very little about your grandmother's religious life.

As the child of pious parents, and as the subject of much biblical instruction at home and in the

16 *

church, it was to be expected that her thoughts would often ascend to the Father of her spirit.

At school her reflections were not unlike those of most intelligent and carefully-reared young people of her age. When for the first time she saw a person upon a deathbed, she called it an " awful spectacle," and could not withhold her prayer that God would " make her ready for such a trying hour." So after an evening party, where there had been a great want of spirited conversation, or a great deal of what her companion called " a flatness," she expressed the wish that " subjects would arise in such places interesting to and becoming a rational mind." The natural thirst of her immortality for some object adequate to meet its wants made itself felt at this period of her life—the period when so many aspiring souls feel the need of something grander and nobler than this world can give.

Not until four years after this date, August, 1801, do we hear from her again. And now the thoughts which, as a school-girl of sixteen years of age, came to her just long enough to reveal their beauty and majesty, and then passed away, take up their abode in her, widening her intellect, stimulating her imagination, quickening her conscience, fortifying her will and comforting her heart. She loves the mountains now as they point toward heaven, and admires the glory of the evening skies. "In the solitude of the stage-coach" she "finds an opportunity for contemplating nature," sees "flowers and trees answering the end for which they were made," and wonders and is sorry "that the noblest part of creation, to which all else is subservient, should neither know nor perform the part for which it is designed." Very decidedly does she express in the diary from which we are quoting, her sense of the insufficiency of any temporal joy to meet the deeper wants of her spirit. She shrinks from "seeking gratification in objects which I already find are as inadequate to satisfy the cravings of an immortal mind as husks are to satisfy the natural appetite." Nor does she hesitate to aver that "without religion in the soul there is a void which nothing else can fill."

Indeed there is dawning in her the existence and beauty of the Kingdom of God. "Lord fill my soul with thy love," is now her prayer. And when asked "whether she would wish to be religious were there no future state?" she answered, "Yes; there appears to be a fitness in serving and glorifying the God of heaven and earth, my great Creator, Preserver and bountiful Benefactor. There is a happiness in it which I hope and wish ever to enjoy." Nor did she desire this blessedness only

for herself. When "the rain was falling refresh-
ingly upon the earth," she writes, "Oh that the
Lord would grant showers of divine grace on the
hearts of the people!" About this time she expresses very deep interest in an account given by
a neighboring clergyman of the conversion of a
number of persons in his congregation, especially in
the new life of a little boy of ten years of age.

"Oh, that, encouraged by this," she writes,
"Christians would be oftener at the throne of grace,
imploring, as a great favor, that God would pour
out his Spirit!" On the day of her brother's ordination, Nov. 5, 1806, she makes this record:

"I feel as if I could joyfully give him up to God,
to be devoted to his service, and to promote his
kingdom in the world."

"The ordination of my dear brother to the pastoral care of this church and congregation binds
him to me with a double tie. He is both my minister and brother."

Her desire now was to come into the closest possible relations with the Redeemer. "Why this
remaining unbelief? Why this fear? Why do I
not come and cast myself on Jesus, believe on him,
hope in his mercy?" "May I receive Christ into
my heart, and enjoy sweet and holy communion
with him!"

" May I see my way clear to make a public profession of his name!" She seeks her dear brother
again, and he encourages her. What transpired in
those conversations is not recorded. She alludes to
them : " Had a conversation with my brother. Gave
him an account of my feelings. Told him I had a
faint hope. He had hopes of me. But I would not
take encouragement from this. I ought not to trust
to man's judgment. O Lord, help me! I would
look into my own heart and search it. By the rules
of thy Word I would compare myself, and know
what manner of person I am." With trembling step
she advances. The glory of the Lord appears at
times, and the sense of his favor. " How sweet,
how endearing, how comforting, how quickening,
is it to unite in singing the praises of our God!"
Then on another day a cloud comes : " Why am I
thus unbelieving? Why these doubts? Why separated from God, from communion with him? It is
sin. This body of sin and death within me, when
will it be destroyed? There are sins hidden from
my view by my own blindness. O Lord, tear them
from my heart, however painful the separation, so
that by any means I may enjoy the display of thy
glory and beauty to my mind; and especially the
light of thy reconciled face." And her prayer is
granted. December comes. The divine Spirit

again takes of the things of Christ and shows them
unto her.   " I never felt more ardent love to Christ,
more fervent desire to be like him; to be conformed
to his image, to serve and glorify him with my
whole heart." Nor does she lose sight of the Lord's
Supper, and the sacred espousal, and mysterious
unition comprehended in it; on the contrary, her eye
is steadily upon it, as was that of the ancient Israelite
on the Holy of Holies. " Dedicated to God in baptism, I feel my covenant obligation; I wish to renew
this, and dedicate myself to him."

With this month of the year 1806 her diary
closes.   But her heart is moving on to the sacrament. On the last leaf but one she writes : " Christ
has said, ' Come unto me, all ye that labor and are
heavy-laden.'   ' For salvation he has provided a
glorious way; a way exactly fitted for such a help-
less creature as I am.' " And then, as if in her mind
receiving and resting upon the Redeemer as he is
freely offered in the Gospel, she says : " O Lord
Jesus, I come; laden with sins, I come; pollutions
have stained my guilty soul, yet if thou wilt, thou
canst make me clean; my Lord and my God, I
believe." " The all-cleansing fountain of thy blood
is sufficient. The way of atonement is full and
clear. Here would I rest. On nothing in my
heart can I for one moment rely. I cast myself on

Jesus Christ, reconciled and delighted." "May the Sun of Righteousness shine into my soul."

During the next year, 1807, she united with the Church.

" He has induced my heart publicly, and I hope sincerely, to set my seal to his covenant of grace, and unreservedly to dedicate myself to him as the *supreme* portion of my soul," is her statement.

If the feelings which have been recorded were of the Holy Spirit, superinducing a new, even a divine life in her soul, making her " accepted in the Beloved—to the praise of the glory of His grace who predestinated her to the adoption of a child," then it was to be expected that her after years would ripen and reveal the fruit of such an election. Nor in this was there any disappointment.

As early as July 24, 1807, she writes to Mr. H. : " I think it must greatly rejoice your heart, as I trust it does in some measure my own, that God is encouraging you to expect that he is about to carry on a work of grace among the people of your charge. I hope that instead of considering yourself as ' in the way,' you will be encouraged to exertion in so glorious a cause as that of the welfare of precious and immortal souls."

At a later period she writes : " I thank you for the pleasing intelligence you give me respecting the

dear people of your charge; dear I hope they may
ever be to each of our hearts, and that I may lend
you every possible assistance of which my feeble
endeavors are capable, and you be the means of
feeding their souls with the bread of life."

And again: " I see how much your heart is set
upon them; I can participate with you in any
pleasing appearances attending them or yourself."
" That the Spirit of God would make the word
effectual to the conversion of many is my ardent desire." Often does she speak now of the " dis-
tinguishing goodness of a merciful and long-suffer-
ing God;" and in January, 1808, she wishes Mr.
H. " a happy new year;" " very happy;" she soon
adds—" happy in much calm, serene, sweet communion with God, which is joy and peace to the soul."

With her characteristic humility, she looks forward with trembling to the burdens that "she ought
to and must soon assume." " I am so unworthy,
sometimes it almost sinks my spirit to think of
them." " But," she adds, " by divine assistance I
hope to be strengthened." If what we are quoting
seems to give too sombre a view of life for one an-
ticipating a bridal very soon, it must be remembered
that we are now looking at the *religious* life of your
grandmother; and that we may not lay before any
eye the wealth of sentiment and affection that gives a

rare value to these early letters. Besides, it was the well-established and often-expressed conviction of your grandparents that a full and abounding enjoyment of God, instead of detracting aught from the choicest gratifications to be found in the rational pleasures of time, only adds to them by augmenting the capacities of our human nature, whilst it regulates and simplifies its thirsts.

"That we may 'mark the hand of our heavenly Father, and thus so live that we may most exquisitely relish the blessings of the world,' as you expressed it, is my most ardent wish," was the form in which her own hand recorded her assent to a profound philosophy, and her faith in the God who made heaven and earth. And then is added, "That we may 'live as we ought'— as fellow-citizens of the New Jerusalem, and fellow-travelers to it—is the prayer of your affectionate friend."

In April, 1808, Miss Sophia Porter was married to Rev. Heman Humphrey by her brother, Rev. Noah Porter. Already had the grounds around the house at Fairfield been laid out and adorned with more than usual care. He who so often calls her his "greatest earthly treasure" had done what he could to prepare the place for one whom he ever after delighted to honor; and Nature withheld not her aid. "The grass begins to look green for

17   N

you," Mr. H. writes on the 30th of March; "I have been trimming the trees; the birds sing among the branches, and seem to say that they will tune their voices to sweeter notes when Sophia comes. Everything seems to smile around our intended habitation.

"The thoughts of your coming to enjoy these pleasant things adds tenfold charms to them even now. How charming will they be when you shall have arrived! There is room for the exercise of a little taste, and I would give more for yours than my own. The present garden-plot is laid out into squares, the alleys of which are lined with rows of English box. I told you about the two evergreen trees in front of the house. I intend to set out the woodbine near them. Some of my friends would fain persuade me that they wish to have you come almost as much as I do. They will not, however, convince me of that."

Thus welcomed, the young bride left Farmington, and her brother's society, and her father's and mother's house, and came to the habitation prepared for her by one who never ceased to give thanks that she had been persuaded to do so. And the piety which shone so beautifully in her mother's house, lost none of its brightness in her own.

It manifested itself in the spirit with which she

made that sacred home so useful, so happy. Generous, because she could not be otherwise, when the love of God intensified this original impulse of her nature, it burned with new lustre and with too costly a flame. Her husband knew it, and has recorded his testimony. And so, had they the opportunity, would those young people and students of Divinity, to whom, by her personal exertions and the free hospitality of her house, she secured an education. Nor was it only in the house that her renovated affection found subjects for its exercise. The people of the towns in which she lived and the students of the college felt it. One of these writes: " She sent to me, when in college, a book called ' Decapolis,' with a little note, containing a request that I would accept it from her, and expressing a wish for my best welfare; the impression from that note and that book never left me." How large the number is that would bear witness in similar form to her desires for their permanent and highest happiness! She loved the Church also. It was her delight to " minister to the saints;" to make the bread and prepare the wine for the communion table, and to mend the clothing of the indigent. Deep in the hearts of young men whose means were limited, and whose friends were few, is her name and memory engraved.

Entering thus readily and largely into Christian labors, she grew more and more into the self-abnegating spirit of the Master, and into the image of His holy temper and sympathies.

Nowhere did this manifest itself more than in her patience and in her gratitude. She had, of course, much to irritate and annoy, as have all mothers and housekeepers, from the infidelities of the service, the constancy and magnitude of the demands, and the difficulties of supply where the household is numerous. But in addition to these not uncommon infelicities, there came upon her in mature life a calamity which deprived her of the joy and strength and ease of apprehension that belonged to all around her. What would she not have given could she, from the fortieth year of her age until her death, have readily distinguished the voices of her friends, her children, her husband, her servants, as in utterance they addressed her! But she could not. In the midst of her years her hearing was impaired. And with what an intelligent and beseeching look did she often search the countenances and watch the lips of those around her, in the hope that she might extract from their faces the meaning of their words! How often, too, did she have to turn that expressive face away in disappointment, and direct those eyes in gentle sadness to the ground! But with what patience did she bear it! Instead of complaining that those around her did not exert themselves and thus make her hear (as often they could not), she retired from their presence to her plain and homely labors, and found her solace in toiling for them. Under this chastisement her soul grew strong for the endurance of heavy sorrows. She was compelled to see Henry die in his early manhood; and John and James and Mary in the midst of life; as before this she had buried two young daughters. On these occasions she never uttered a murmuring word, and scarcely spoke aloud her grief. Her eyes filled with tears, and she went about her duties in quietness, with her head somewhat bowed, as if saying, " The Lord gave and the Lord hath taken away." It was so also when your grandfather was taken sick. The tokens of pain upon her features as she stood and looked at him and took his hand, unable, as he cast his last look upon her, to catch the words which in weakness he articulated, seemed to say, If it be possible let this cup pass away; but after kneeling by his bedside, and then rising and ministering—ministering, toiling —toiling on, for anybody's relief but her own, there came over her face the expression that never afterward entirely left it, of " Not my will, but thine be done."

17 *

After this your grandmother continued with us in the enjoyment of good health, for a person of her age, for seven years and eight months.

She took pleasure in seeing her friends; went as before to the house of God; received her children and children's children at her own home; shared in their joys; took a deep interest in their usefulness; and approached the close of her earthly journey with the serenity and ripening glow with which spring and summer merge their days of seed-time and promise into the autumn of golden fruits and grateful songs.

On Sunday, the 6th of December, 1868, she was prevented in consequence of a severe cold, from going to the sanctuary. Soon she laid down upon her couch, and then, early in the evening, retired to her bed. From this bed she never rose. Her disease became acute bronchitis. An excellent physician and kind friends came to her; her two remaining daughters never left her side; she continued to grow weaker, but sang her song in the night from a hymn that had become a favorite with her, as well it might:

> "Then shall I hear, and see, and know
> All I desired or hoped below."

Nor did anticipations alone fill her mind. Gratitude and words of penitence came from her lips.

On one day it was " Lord, have mercy on me a sinner;" on the next, thankfulness for favors in the past took possession of her; until at length in the very language in which, sixty years before, she had expressed her sense of the loving-kindness of God when looking forward to her earthly bridal, she now distinctly articulated : "What shall I render unto the Lord for all his benefits to me?" as she moved on to the marriage-supper of the Lamb.

Having been taken sick on the Sabbath, she continued through the days of the following week to entertain—and in her occasional bewilderment, to express—the desire that she might go to church. And she was not disappointed. On Sunday, the 13th of December, 1868, soon after the church bells in Pittsfield had ceased to ring, she left these earthly scenes, no longer shut out from the sweet melodies of sound, to hear the music, and join in the worship of the skies.

And may it not be that the voice which once welcomed her so affectionately to the home prepared for her on earth, lifted itself up again in thanksgiving and praise, with that of her brother, and of each child who had gone before, as the Master of Assemblies bade her welcome to the place he had prepared for her in the mansions of the blessed?

H. N.

PITTSFIELD, *April*, 1869.